The Hand That's Dealt

By

Rosalind Coats

This book is a work of fiction. Places, events, and situations in this story are purely fictional. Any resemblance to actual persons, living or dead, is coincidental.

ISBN: 1-4033-2889-7 (E-book)
ISBN: 1-4033-2890-0 (Paperback)

This book is printed on acid free paper.

1stBooks - rev. 11/05/02

This book is dedicated to the memory of Curtis and Gradie Coats. (my grandparents)
Two of the most motivational and inspirational people ever.

Special Thanks: To my parents Robert and Camille Coats for doing what they thought was right, even when I thought it was wrong.

To my brothers: Robert Lee Jr., Mark Anthony Sr., Marlin Andrew, and Markell Allen, for lending me their strength to fall back on and shoulders to stand on to see my way.

To my sisters: Romona Lynn, Rochell Louise, and Rayna Marie, for all their support and encouragement to make me go after a dream I was too afraid to admit I had.

To the whole Coats Family, ya'll know it's too many to mention, that would be another book…hmmm…One Love!

Finally and most important Thanks be to God.

….I see you Janesse and B.J.

Victoria Dupree, young, beautiful, and ambitious, on the verge of starting her own independent life.

She has a wonderful family and a number one ace Shan. However, her love life is in the dumps.

Thomas is in love with her and she's in love with James who is only in love with himself. Things start,

To look up in the relationship department when she meets Eric. But loving Eric is causing her to,

Loose relationships at home and with her best friend. In her fray to make Eric love her the way she,

Loves him, she looses her best friend, the one man who has always truly loved her, and her will to,

Go on. Will Vicki find what it is she believes will make her happy, and what cost is she willing to pay?

Lives, and relationships at stake, will Vicki come out on top,

Playing *THE HAND THAT'S DEALT?*

This book is dedicated to the memory of Curtis and Gradie Coats. (my grandparents)
Two of the most motivational and inspirational people ever.

Special Thanks: To my parents Robert and Camille Coats for doing what they thought was right, even when I thought it was wrong.

To my brothers: Robert Lee Jr., Mark Anthony Sr., Marlin Andrew, and Markell Allen, for lending me their strength to fall back on and shoulders to stand on to see my way.

To my sisters: Romona Lynn, Rochell Louise, and Rayna Marie, for all their support and encouragement to make me go after a dream I was too afraid to admit I had.

To the whole Coats Family, ya'll know it's too many to mention, that would be another book…hmmm…One Love!

Finally and most important Thanks be to God.

….I see you Janesse and B.J.

Victoria Dupree, young, beautiful, and ambitious, on the verge of starting her own independent life.

She has a wonderful family and a number one ace Shan. However, her love life is in the dumps.

Thomas is in love with her and she's in love with James who is only in love with himself. Things start,

To look up in the relationship department when she meets Eric. But loving Eric is causing her to,

Loose relationships at home and with her best friend. In her fray to make Eric love her the way she,

Loves him, she looses her best friend, the one man who has always truly loved her, and her will to,

Go on. Will Vicki find what it is she believes will make her happy, and what cost is she willing to pay?

Lives, and relationships at stake, will Vicki come out on top,

Playing *THE HAND THAT'S DEALT?*

CHAPTER 1

Vicki sat at the kitchen table painting her nails a fire engine red. She looked out the kitchen window into the backyard she spent years playing in with her brother Vernon. They use to think it was so big. They would race, skate, ride bikes; she even got him to turn her jump rope with the other end tied to the fence. She noticed her mothers rose garden and her thoughts quickly left the past and shot to the present. She was all grown up now. Those roses reminded her of the ones James surprised her with last night. James was the man Vicki preferred to spend all of her time with. She had other male friends, but James was the number one. She really only got to spend time with him when it was convenient for him. James would never admit that though, but both he and Vicki knew it was true. She got up and got a bag of cookies from the cabinet. She poured herself a glass of milk, and sat back down at the table to think more on James. Before she could dip her first cookie in the milk her brother Vernon walked in. "That's why you fat now, with ya greedy ass." She rolled her eyes at Vernon and twisted her lips. He went to the refrigerator and poured himself a glass of juice. He drank it down in one long gulp. She wasn't bothered by Vernon's comment. She knew he was just playing, and she knew she wasn't fat. She has a shape that most women would die for literally. Vicki was about 135lbs, and at the height of 5'4" she knew she had it going on. That insult was just Vernon's way of letting her know he thought the same. She went on dipping her cookies in her milk. "Vicki, let me get five." Vicki held up five fingers to Vernon then twisted her hand around and gave him the middle finger. "Come on, you know you gone be asking to borrow my truck or something from me." She knew he wasn't telling a lie; she loved to drive his truck. "Go get it off my nightstand, and not a penny more, with yo' broke ass. How you go to work every night and all the time broke? What are you doing with your money?" "It's what I'm not doing, plus Brenda ass be breaking me, hollering the baby need something every twenty minutes, and got the nerve to be on the fucking county." Vicki just shook her head and watched Vernon leave the kitchen. He really is trying to be straight on the up and up. Having a baby has calmed him down a lot. Vicki loved his little girl

Veronica. She just wished it wasn't by that hood rat Brenda. But that is what Vernon gets for being out there like he was. Vicki let her thoughts go back to high school when the phone rang. She almost ran to the phone expecting it to be James. They had spent the night together in one of the most fancy hotels in San Francisco. When he dropped her off this morning, he promised to call her and come back and get her for dinner. Now here it was almost six-thirty and he still hasn't called. She answered the phone with high hopes, SHATTERED. It was Brenda. "I hate this bitch," Vicki whispered to herself but hoped Brenda heard her. Brenda had sucked her teeth and asked for Vernon. "He ain't here." Vicki hung up the phone before Brenda could respond. So what if Vernon was there. Brenda shouldn't be trying to dog her brother out. As soon as Vicki hung up the phone she paged James. After fifteen minutes of waiting the phone finally rang. "Hey there sexy girl." James really knew how to get Vicki to smile. "What's up James?" was all she could come up with. After waiting all day to talk to him Vicki realized she didn't have a thing to say. Just hearing his smooth baritone voice was enough for her. "Not much baby girl. I was just about to get to a phone and call you when you paged me. I know we were supposed to go eat, but I got caught up. So look here let me get at you later." They hung up the phone. James was like a drug and Vicki had just gotten her fix. Ever since high school she has had the biggest crush on James Roberts. He was a senior and she was a freshman. Vernon made sure that no one paid Vicki any attention let alone King Highs most known player. Not that he noticed Vicki any way. He was dating the captain of the cheer leading team, and about twelve other girls, not including the ones that didn't even go to King. When she was a senior and Vernon and James had long since graduated, she ran into James in the mall. They exchanged numbers and have been seeing each other off and on ever since. Mostly off because Vicki wasn't giving up the goods. Now they have what James calls an open relationship. Free to see other people but always keeping each other first. Vicki kept up her end, and well she was working on James. Sooner or later she would wear him down. She always tried to convince herself of that. Which is what she was doing when her mother walked in the front door with two bags.

"Hey ma, you want to go shoot some pool?" She asked as she took the bags out of her mother's arms. " No not tonight Vicki, me and your daddy are going out tonight." Vicki had a surprised look on her face. "Well I'll be, you mean he hitting the streets and taking you with him this time. Well, well, must be a blue moon." Her and her mother started laughing. "Hush up Vicki, ain't no blue moon, but did you just see that pig fly by?" They started laughing hysterically. Vernon came into the kitchen. "What is so funny?" They both looked at him and kept laughing. "Well laugh on, sounding like cackling hens." He kissed his mother on the cheek and headed out for work. Vicki went to the living room and decided to call Thomas. Everyone had something to do this Saturday night except Vicki. Thomas had a real thing for Vicki. He was fine, he loved to spend money, and that black BMW that he sometimes let Vicki borrow was just the icing on the cake. He worked at Lardens department store, as a manager. But everybody knew that was just a front. He was one of the Bay Areas biggest dope dealers. "Yeah" when Thomas answered the phone it made Vicki cringe. It wasn't that he was bad to be with; its just he hounded her. He was always complaining about her not being only with him, and accusing her of boning someone else. It likes to drive her crazy him being so obsessive over something that wasn't even his. "Hey Thomas" Vicki was trying to sound sweet, she wanted Thomas to come and get her. "Oh now you could call a nigga, after you been out all night giving that ass to the next man." Here we go she thought. Now she wished she had never called him at all. "You coming to get me or not?" She cut straight to the point, and ignored his snide remark. It was a desperate attempt not to go down the same tired road with Thomas yet again. Thomas let out a slight laugh. "Give me thirty minutes, girl you gone drive me crazy you know that." "I know but you love it" In thirty minutes Thomas was there. That was one of the things Vicki appreciated about Thomas, he was always on time, and always followed through. She smiled on her way out the door as she passed the roses James gave her. Since he was busy tonight, Thomas would have to do.

CHAPTER 2

Monday mornings were Vicki's worst. She didn't really hate her job; it was the getting up at six-thirty to make it there by eight o'clock. She worked as an administrative assistant for an architecture firm. The job was helping to put her through school. Around five years ago she started working there through a summer youth program. She was invited back to work every summer since then. When school was in she worked two days out of the week. Before she could get one foot in the door the phone was ringing. "Wrigler Bryant and associates, how can I help you". It was Thomas. "I'm taking you to lunch." "Thomas, what the hell you calling this early in the morning. I haven't even got my coat of yet. I'll call you later." She hung up on Thomas before he could respond. That was one the things she hated about Thomas. She would spend some time with him, and he would get to assuming he owned her. She didn't know why she put up with him sometimes. Honestly she didn't know why he put up with her. She was so mean to him some times. Only because she knew she could get away with it. One day, she thought to herself, Thomas isn't going to be there for her. She quickly dismissed that thought when she looked at the gold bracelet he got for her.

She went into the employee lounge and began to start the coffeepot. These white folk drank coffee all day long she thought to herself. Just then Mr. Wrigler walked in. He was Randolph Wrigler of Wrigler Bryant and Associates. "Good morning Victoria, I'll take two sugars and no cream, sweet and black just like you". He winked his eye at her and laughed at his own ignorance and went into his office. He always had some kind of dumb comment to say. Like once they were having a conversation about Oprah Winfrey. They were trying to figure out what her mans name was. He says oh ask Victoria she must know. Of course Vicki knew who he was with his fine self. She didn't give them the satisfaction. She shrugged her shoulder and said she didn't have a clue. Said she wasn't even an Oprah fan. Knowing full well she taped the show everyday. As she was bringing the coffee over to Mr. Wriglers office, Bobbie White came in. She was the Office manager, and the one who suggested Vicki comes back every summer. "Vicki, the package on your desk needs to go down to Jacob's and Sons, please, it needs to be there by nine-thirty." Jacobs and Sons architecture firm was about four blocks away. Vicki often ran packages or drawings over to them. "I'll go ahead and take them now, we are going to be pretty busy later". She grabbed the package off her desk and headed out the door. When she got to the office Mr. Jacobs was out, but his son was in. "Good morning beautiful." When he spoke, Vicki's stomach did a somersault. She had hardly expected a voice like that to come out of the mouth of such a fair skinned brother. It was even deeper than James was. Vicki cleared her throat. "Good morning, is Mr. Jacobs available, or his secretary Linda?" "No they are not, but I'm available" he looked down at Vicki with those green eyes and he smiled at her with them. Vicki thought that to be a hook line, and she was definitely going to bite. She gave him what she thought was a sexy smile and narrowed her eyes and said "Available for what?" She felt like kicking herself after she said it. It was so corny, and way to forward even for her. He suddenly got this bewildered look on his face. "Available to collect the drawings you are here to drop off, you are Victoria right?" Vicki just stared at him and wished the world would end. "Bobbie called and said you were on your way. You can just leave them on the table." Vicki's mouth dropped open. He pushed the bottom of his chin up in an effort to motion her to close her mouth and he walked out of the room. Vicki felt like a fool. That pompous jerk Vicki thought as she walked out of the office. She had never felt so humiliated.

When she got back to her own office, it was in full swing. She went over to Lita Phillips desk and told her about the incident. "Yeah Vicki, I've seen him at conferences, I have to admit the man is fine, but he has an arrogant air about himself." Lita was one of the coolest white women that Vicki knew. She didn't know many, but she couldn't imagine them being as cool as Lita. She grew up in South Central Los Angels, she was excepted to UCLA but the scholarship wasn't nearly enough to cover the cost. She worked two jobs, and graduated on the dean's list. She was hired through a recruiting program, and had more talent than any man in the business. "Damn Lita, he totally embarrassed me." They went on talking about him for a few more minutes then got back to work. It was going to be a long day.

Friday, five o'clock, couldn't get there soon enough. When Vicki got home there was a message on the memo pad to call Shan. Shan was Vicki's best friend. Shan lived across the street with her son Marcus. Vicki and Shan met through Vernon. Him and Shan had a so-called relationship. Vicki picked up the phone and called Shan. "What's up ho?" Shan started laughing. "I'm getting paid though', Vicki I know you going out with me tonight. There is this new club downtown around two blocks from your job. Its called *Flashlights*." Shans favorite pass time next to men was going out. Vicki loved to go out with Shan because she really knew how to have a good time. "Yes Shan count me in, what's the dress code? I'm not going to no wild ass eighteen and over, sweatsuits and boots, hats, gats, and baseball bats, club like you had me in last Saturday night." Shan started laughing. "Vicki you have no sense. It wasn't that bad. But no this is twenty-one and over, it's new and the dress code is top notch baby, and strictly enforced."

"Okay Shan, what time do I need to be ready?" "Be ready around ten-thirty, I'll blow: Vicki started laughing and said, "I bet you say that to all the guys." "Only if they fine bitch". They hung up. Shan was twenty-four the same age as Vernon. Her son Marcus was six, and his father was killed in a car accident around four years ago. For two years after his death Shan confined herself to her apartment. She would only leave to cash her welfare checks. She even ordered her groceries. Then one-day Vernon got hold to her. After she stopped messing with Vernon it was no stopping her. She though she was the diva of all divas. Nobody could tell her anything. And if you tried she would curse you out so bad you would just bow your head, tuck your tail and walk away. Vicki thought she was bad messing with James and Thomas, but Shan had her beat. Three, sometimes four different guys a week. None of them lasts more than two months. If you weren't doing something for Shan or her son then you could get to stepping. Whenever they wanted to get serious with Shan, she would give them the walking papers. That is what happened with Vernon, he wanted to tie her down. Now him and Shan are good friends. Shan is

what most brothers; men period would call top notch fine. There was so much more to her than her appearance, but she didn't work those assets. Like her natural ability to do hair. Vicki tried encouraging Shan to go to cosmetology school so she could do hair professionally. She would start and go a few weeks, get bored and up and quit. But that was Shan, can't commit to anything.

At ten-thirty Shan was outside blowing. Vicki wore her long black spandex tube dress with the split up the side and some platform black sandals. Her hair was in braids, braided in a bob style that Shan done two weeks ago and they still looked brand new. Of course Shan was styling. She had her hair in a very short hair cut like Toni Braxton before her weave. She was wearing a gold shiny mini skirt, with a half top to match and some gold strap pumps. The only person in the world Vicki thought could wear gold lipstick and look good was Shan. Vicki went out and got in the car and they were off for another night of partying and drinking. Shan was right about the club being two blocks from Vicki's job they passed it on the way to the club and again while they were looking for a parking space. They finally got in after twenty minutes of looking for a parking space, and another thirty minutes standing in line. The club was very nice Vicki had to admit. Not like the usual hole in the walls Shan usually found. It had an upstairs for you to just sit, drink and socialize with a live jazz band. You walked down into the club where the dance floor was. As they walked down the stairs the music came blasting through the stairway. They were playing Gangsta Party, by Tupac; Shan had to get right in Vicki's face in order to hear her. "Vicki I'm headed for the bar, the first drinks are on me. You drinking your usual kamikaze?" Vicki thought about switching up then changed her mind. "Yeah, make sure it's straight up." Vicki and Shan danced and drank and drank and danced, they were having a really good time. They sat at the bar sipping on another drink that Shan talked some buck tooth guy with gold caps on the front of his grill into buying them before she sent him on his way, when a man that could have passed for Denzel Washington's twin came towards them. Shan didn't waste any time. "Mine Vicki, so don't even think about it." He was fine, and if he tried to talk to her, Vicki thought she was going for it. To hell with Shan, all is fair. He walked over and spoke to both of them. "I'm Jason, how are you both enjoying yourselves?" Before Vicki could blink, Shan jumped in. Well I personally would be having much more fun if we could hit the dance floor." He smiled and looked a little embarrassed at her straight forwardness, but quickly recovered. "That was my intent Ms.Lady, let's do this." They took off to the dance floor and Sexual Healing by Marvin Gaye came on, instead of sitting at the bar looking lonely Vicki decided to go to the bathroom. It was packed and smelled like cheap perfume. She went back to her seat at the bar and turned her barstool around so that her back was to the dance floor. Cool Water, Vicki thought to herself as some man walked up behind her. He was wearing one of Vicki's favorite colognes for men. She almost turned around to comment, but being bold was Shan's thing and the one time she did try it earlier in the week, she ended up standing in some office with her mouth hanging open. "If you look as good from the front as you do from behind I have to have this dance." Damn he sounded fine, Vicki thought, but his approach was off and if that is the best pick up line he could come up with, he can keep stepping'. Vicki took a deep breath, turned around with the intent of declining his request. Besides she never slow danced with strangers any way. When she was turned around she was staring into the smile of a god. It was him, the finest man she never got. She had to remind herself to close her mouth before he did. She had opened it to say something but when she saw Eric Jacobs nothing came out. He saved her. "Oh hello Victoria, the cat still got your tongue? Come on let's dance." She took a deep breath, and a moment to collect herself. "Mr.Jacobs, nice to see you, but no thank you". She felt good turning him down. She knew he didn't encounter too much of that. She wanted to dance with him; she would have paid a month salary to be next to him on a slow grind. She ad to play it off. He gave a half a smile. "All right, now we are even. So you feel better, let's dance." He took her by the hand and led her to the dance floor. She didn't resist. As soon as the got to the floor, the song went off. Vicki thought to herself if she had had a gun she would have shot the deejay. In Between the sheets, by the Isley Brothers came on right behind it. Vicki thanked the stars for it. They were singing that song and Vicki let her imagination run wild. This man was fine. He whispered in her ear. "You feel so good, let this be me and you baby." When he ran his tongue over her ear her thoughts shot back to the club and her eyes popped open. She was getting beside herself. He was massaging her back and whispering in her ear. She started to feel nervous. The song went off and *Gotta Get You Home* by Foxy Brown came on. This was too much Vicki thought. He let her out of his arms, and they begin to dance. Vicki looked up into those green eyes that were smiling down at her. She looked past Eric and was staring right into the face of James. Some girl walked by and he asked her to dance. They came and danced right next to Eric and Vicki. They were freaking and rubbing all over each other like they were some where in private. Vicki was beginning to get agitated. She grabbed Eric by the hand and thanked him for the dance. She was about to walk off the dance floor and he rubbed the side of her face, cupped her chin in his hand and bent his head forward and kissed her. He made his tongue familiar with the inside of her mouth like it belonged there. When he pulled back he pecked her one, last, soft kiss on the lips. "Let's get out of here." Vicki didn't give it a second thought. She was headed hand in hand out of the club with Eric. Shan was calling Vicki but she didn't hear her. Somebody grabbed her arm, it was James. "Vicki, don't you hear yo' friend calling you. That's who you came with, that's who you need to be leaving with." Eric looked from Vicki to James, then back at Vicki. "Who is this your father?" Eric started laughing. James looked like a little boy compared to Eric. Eric stood around 6'2" and carried about 220lbs+ very well. James was about 5'8" and his 170lbs if that made him look pretty tiny next to Eric. Vicki could tell by the look on James face that nothing was funny. Before he went into his gangster role Vicki jumped in. "Uh, Eric this is my, well uh" she didn't know how to introduce James this is her what… "James, this is Eric, Eric, James." Eric held his hand out to James. "How you doing man?" James looked at Eric's extended hand then over at Vicki, then back to Eric. He knotted up his face and walked off. Vicki was so embarrassed. Shan walked over and filled in the embarrassing silence. "Vicki, where were you going, I have the keys." Vicki looked at Shan and then motioned her eyes for Shan to look at Eric. A huge grin crossed Shan's face. "Oh I see, well can you at least walk me to the car. You know all the sickos we have in the city." Shan held her hand out to Eric. "Hi, I'm ShanTanette, and you are?" He shook her hand. "I'm Eric, pleased to meet you, ShanTanette. We'll make sure you get to your car, where did you park?" Shan was flirting with Eric, just grinning all up at him and was still holding on to his hand. Vicki answered, "you can call her Shan, and we parked around two blocks up". Vicki nudged Shan in her side to get her to quit staring at Eric. "Well I had valet, so come on let's go." When the driver pulled up in Eric's red Lexus, Shan pinched the inside of Vicki's arm. He opened the door for Vicki and Shan and while Eric was walking around to the driver side Shan whispered form the back seat, "You better work it girl." They were trying to suppress their giggles when he got into the car. "Must be talking about me, That's okay." He leaned over and kissed Vicki on her cheek. "You are so beautiful Victoria." They dropped Shan off at her car and were off.

The alcohol and heat had Vicki sleep before they got to the freeway. When she opened her eyes, she was in an underground parking lot. He got out the car and ran around to her side and opened her door. Vicki thought to herself how James never did classy things like that. They walked hand and hand over to a set of elevators. The garage was cold, and along with her uneasiness, Vicki began to tremble. "You cold Victoria?" He took his suit coat off and draped it over her shoulders. These elevators can be so slow." He stood behind her, and stated rubbing her arms. Then he moved to her breast. He was circling her nipples with his thumbs and kissing her neck and the side of her face. Just as she felt something trickle between her legs the elevator doors opened. It made her jump. She stated thinking about James, how she knew he was in front of her house or paging her. She thought about Thomas and how sweet he really was and how she never really gave him a real chance. She thought about how the very man who was holding her and kissing her, was the same pompous jerk who made a complete fool of her earlier this week. She started losing her nerve. He must have sensed her hesitation; he hugged her tightly from behind. As they rode up to the fifteenth floor. They stepped out of the elevator and walked a couple of steps to apartment 1504. He opened the door and motioned for her to go in first. "Make yourself at home Victoria." The apartment was plush. When you walk in you are in a small hallway. You take a few steps and to the left was the kitchen. It didn't look like a pot of water had been boiled in it, let alone a meal cooked. Straight ahead and to the right was the living room. In the middle of the living room was a nice Oriental rug. On top was a glass table with black legs and gold trim. He had black leather sofa and love seat, and a huge leather recliner. An entertainment center that covered the entire wall. He had African art on the wall. Everything looked so tasteful. Vicki was impressed. Vicki made her way to the couch. Eric came out of the kitchen. "No not there, in here." He pointed to the end of the hallway at what Vicki assumed to be the bedroom. Vicki pointed to the cordless phone on the end table. "I need to use the phone." He tilted his head to the side and narrowed his eyes at her in curiosity. "Are you all right Victoria?" Vicki swallowed hard. She wanted to say no, and ask Eric to take her home.

"I'm fine, I just need to call Shan and make sure she made it home. We had a lot to drink tonight." He let a huge grin cross his lips. It looked as if God himself placed each tooth in that man's mouth. "You have to check in with your uh, uh, James?" Vicki laughed at Eric teasing her about earlier. "No, honestly, I just want to check on Shan." He walked over to her and pulled her in an embrace. "Well, there happens to be a phone in the bedroom, pretty convenient wouldn't you say?" She smiled and hugged him back as she buried her face deeper into his chest and sniffed his sexy scent. "Yes Eric, very convenient." He led her into the bedroom. When she walked in she got butterflies. He had a king size bed, with a dark green satin comforter, and black and green throw pillows. Two nightstands stood on both sides of the bed and the room had a walk in closet. There was a dresser in the corner of the room and it was covered with papers, a television, a laptop computer, and several different bottles of smell goods. Vicki sat on the edge of the bed and dialed Shan number. "Shan this is Vicki, you made it home safely." "Vicki, James is outside, he was parked there when I pulled up. He got a lot of nerve for somebody that ain't yo' man." "Who you telling, he is the one who wanted to be free, so I don't know what he be tripping for. I knew he was going to do that. Damn, what should I do?" "What are you tripping for, you need to do that fine ass nigga you with. James can see who ever he wants to right, so you can do the same. Where is Eric anyway?" "He is in the shower, look it just stopped so I have to go. I'll call you tomorrow." She hung up the phone with Shan just as Eric walked out of the bathroom. He was still wet with a towel wrapped around his waist. "You want to take a shower Victoria, I'll give you something to sleep in." He opened his drawer and handed her black forty-niners T-shirt. Eric walked Vicki to the bathroom and stood against the wall and watched her as she closed the door. Vicki stared at herself in the bathroom mirror. She felt like she was looking at some one else. This couldn't be her, in a strange man's apartment about to go to bed with him. What about all the morals she had, the training and good upbringing and growing up in the church. Granted she was no angle, and hadn't been to church with her mother in a while but this was just not her. She started to get undressed. She wished she could magically zap herself home. She heard Eric singing in between the sheets. Damn the nigga could sing to. She turned the shower on. She looked at her body in the mirror and wondered if Eric would be pleased. She studied herself from every angel until the steam from the shower fogged the mirror. She showered, dried off, and then lotions down with the Victoria Secrets she kept in her purse. When she walked out of the bathroom Eric had all the lights off and candles were burning. He was sitting in the middle of the bed leaning back on one of his elbows. He had a bowl of strawberries and whip cream. When he took his hand from behind his back he had a bottle of wine and two glasses. Vicki couldn't help but smile. He covered everything. She placed her clothes on the floor in the corner. She was stalling, she wasn't sure she wanted to through with this. "Victoria, baby why are you stalling, come here and let daddy relax you." It was like he was reading her mind. "Oh uh, I'm not stalling." She took a deep breath and walked over to him. He poured them both a drink and made a toast. "A toast to a friendship in the making, and may it lead to bigger and better things." They clinked glasses and he picked up a strawberry, dipped it in the cream and fed it to her. Before she took her mouth away she licked around his fingers. Eric put the platter and the glasses on the floor. He started kissing her toes then working his way up her right leg. Vicki anticipated the moves Eric would make. She could tell he knew how to please a woman. She just lay there and let her thoughts wander to night after night of passion with this man. He moistened the inside of her thigh with his tongue, and took one lick around the top of her clitoris, then blew on it. She let out a little gasp. He began to work it like he made it up. She wanted him inside of her badly. He caressed her breast, as he tasted her. He stated kissing around her private area, then her belly button. He stooped and reached over into the nightstand and pulled out a condom. He slid in ever so gently and rocked back and forth slowly. This was the best she ever had. It was going to be the last person she was with, she vowed to herself to make this man hers.

Vicki woke up the next morning in bed by herself. That is when she realized it was afternoon. She pulled her head up and looked around the room for Eric. She got out of bed and hated the way she smelled. Like alcohol and sex. She remembered whom the sex was with and how great it was and started to smile. She went into the bathroom, gargled with some mouthwash, and took a quick shower. She put the T-shirt back on from last night. She looked back in the room for Eric. He wasn't there. She walked into the livingroom and checked the kitchen, no Eric and not even a note. Where the hell was he. He had some nerve leaving her here. How rude she thought. She wanted to get dressed and get the hell out of his apartment, if this even was his apartment. Then she realized she had no idea where she was, and the only clothes she had would not be appropriate for the bus. She decided to make up the bed and wait it out. Just as she was carrying the dishes from last night to the kitchen the front door opened. There he was holding a bouquet of at least two dozen red roses. He smiled and winked one of those beautiful green eyes at her and her heart melted. She knew then that she was in love.

CHAPTER 3

Four weeks passed and no James. Vicki tried paging him several times but just didn't get a response. She couldn't understand what his problem was. He was the one after all who wanted an open relationship. Screw him she thought to herself. She had Eric now and he was more of a man than James Roberts ever hoped to be. Eric and Vicki had been hanging out for the past month. Doing all the things that lovers do. Candle light dinners, long walks in the park and on the beach, movies, skating, and the whole nine yards. She already wanted to introduce him to her mother and father, even Vernon. Only after a month, she felt in her heart that Eric was the one. She decided to give him a call. There was no answer and his machine picked up. She left him a message. "Hi Eric this is Vicki, call me when you get in, miss you." When she hung up she remembered he told her he had a Saturday morning meeting. Seconds after she hung up the phone rang. She though it was Eric maybe he skipped the meeting and was screening his calls. She cleared her throat and answered the phone in a voice she thought was sexy. It was Shan. "Remember me ho" It dawned on Vicki just then that in her weeks of bliss with Eric, she hadn't even bothered to call Shan. "Of course remember my ace, what's up?" Vicki tried to sound sincere, but she sounded guilty, even to herself. "Vicki damn, you are never home. I try paging you but you won't call me back, what's up with that?" Damn Vicki thought. She wanted to tell Shan you aint my man. But it was true she had been so caught up with Eric, that she had been avoiding Shan to keep herself available for him. Not to mention her own family. "Shan it ain't even like that, I just been getting ready for school to start, and work has really been hectic. I tried to call you a few times but I guess we kept missing each other." Vicki held her breath as she waited for Shan to buy her story. "What ever Vicki, I called for Vernon any way, can you put him on the phone please?" Vicki blew her breath and sucked her teeth. She put the phone down to go get Vernon, but not before she heard Shan say some friend, now I don't feel so bad. What ever Shan was talking about Vicki didn't care. Shan was just jealous. Vicki couldn't help it if she found a man and Shan didn't. Shan wasn't about to make her feel bad for spending time with Eric and loving it.

She better get over it. Vicki said out loud hoping that Shan heard her. She walked down the hall to Vernon's room and opened the door. "Vernon telephone" she said as she was opening his room door. He popped his head up and so did Brenda. "What he fu.. Why you didn't knock?" "Well I didn't know you had company, why didn't you lock the door. You know mama don't like this type of stuff Vernon." Vicki knew Brenda hated Shan, but Vicki hated Brenda. "Any way Shan is on the phone for you." Brenda rolled her eyes at Vernon and looked back at Vicki. "And, what do she want?" "Not you Brenda, Vernon need to get out the bed and ask her since that is who she called for." "Vicki, tell her I'll get back at her, now get out and close the door." Vicki knew Vernon was mad and that she would have to pay for this later. So she went on trying to get on Brenda nerves. "Where is the baby, you over here staying the night laying up and Veronica not even here?" Vernon answered as he got out of the bed. He was almost laughing. "She at her grandma house, get the hell out Vicki". He pushed her into the hallway and closed and locked the door. She fell into the wall like he pushed her harder than he did. "Get over it" he yelled through his closed door. She walked back into the living room laughing. She had forgot Shan was on the phone, she picked it up but he line was dead. She rolled her eyes at the phone and thought oh well, she already mad anyway. She pressed the hang up button on the phone and released it and called James. There was no answer. She decided to call Thomas. He answered on the first ring. "Hey Tommy this is Vicki." She tried to sound cheerful. Truth told, if the shoe was on the other foot, she would have hung up on Thomas. "Yeah" Thomas sounded so dry. After hearing his voice she realized how much she really missed him. She knew Thomas was mad at her. She was surprised he wasn't through with her all together. James was mad at her, Shan was mad at her, and she hadn't talked to Thomas in even longer time than those two. "I called to tell you I really miss you Thomas." He let out a little laugh. "Is that right Victoria?" She knew he was mad, that is the only time he called her Victoria. "Can I see you later?" Thomas almost sounded pathetic. She didn't respond. She wanted to wait and see if she would see Eric Later. "Look Vicki, yeah I'm still living if you just tryna see if I am still on hold for you well I ain't gone let you keep me hanging for ever why you run around doing God knows what. So you can just miss me with that missing me shit. I'm out" He hung up the phone in her face. She felt awful. She called him right back. He answered on the first ring. "Yeah" He sounded so mean. "Thomas listen, you didn't give me a chance to respond. It's a little after nine, can you come and get me around noon?" Vicki guessed she did sort of have Thomas on hold. She didn't mean to hurt him in any way. He was a grown man that could make his own decisions. "Look Vicki, don't do me no favors, you not the only person I could spend my Saturday with." She let out a long sigh. "Well I'm the one you want to spend it with, and I want to see you. So are you coming or not. He started laughing. What was it about this girl that had him acting like a punk he thought to himself? "Girl, I'll be there at twelve, but listen you gone miss me when I leave yo' little ass alone." They hung up. She decided to lie down for a while before Thomas came. When she opened her eyes it was 11:20. She jumped up. She knew Thomas would be on time. She grabbed her black Guess jeans that Thomas bought her out of the closet. She got her white button up guess shirt out of the drawer and some white tennis shoes. After she showered and dressed, she was pulling her braids up into a ponytail and heard a knock at the door. She stuck her head out of the bathroom window and told Thomas to come in. He came in and sat on the side of the tub while Vicki finished messing with her braids. "Damn girl you look good." Vicki didn't look at Thomas she just smiled and said thank you, you to. When she finished her hair they walked into Vicki's room. She felt Thomas's eyes glued to her behind. As she was reaching for her jacket he touched her on the butt. "Thomas you better watch yo' self." He studied her closely. "Yo' who been killing my cat?" He had a look on his face like he was expecting her to answer. Before she could think of a smart remark for Thomas's question Vernon walked in the room. "Vicki what you doing keeping company with a hood like this? Thomas stated laughing. He stood up and they gave each other the pound. "What the deal V-Dog, where my money at with yo' little bony ass." He had a pleading look on his face. "Hey let that go T, I get with you on that later. Vicki wanted to know why Vernon owed Thomas money.

She knew what Thomas was into, and what Vernon use to be in to. She hoped Vernon wasn't about to get caught back up in that madness. She made a mental note to ask him later. "Hey Vicki, I thought you said you wasn't fuckin' with Thomas ugly ass no more, since you started kicking it with that cat in the red drop. Didn't you say you were cool on my boy Tom?" Vicki couldn't believe Vernon was trying to bust her out like this. Then she remembered the little Brenda episode from this morning. This was his pay back. Thomas wrinkled up his brow. "What red drop, who, I know you ain't messing with Tyler." Vernon left the room laughing. Tyler was a big time drug dealer in the streets of San Francisco, kind of like Thomas rivalry. They use to be hooked up, but one night a deal went bad and they ended up getting robbed for a lot of money. Thomas thinks Tyler set him up. "Thomas Vernon just playing, I'm not messing with Tyler." He looked suspiciously at Vicki. "Don't get that nigga killed Vicki, I'd have to hurt both y'all assess. Vicki rolled her eyes at Thomas. "Can we leave now?" When they walked outside James was parked right behind Thomas BMW No he wasn't just gone come by with out calling, after he has been ignoring her all this time Vicki thought. James looked at Thomas and Vicki in the doorway. He pressed the alarm on his Maxima, started laughing and jogged across the street to Shan house. Her son opened the door and James picked him up and they went in side. Thomas was already at the car with the door open waiting on Vicki. She was just frozen in the doorway staring at Shan house. Thomas startled her when he spoke. "Vicki you coming or you just gone stand there and stare at yo' partner house?" What was James doing at Shan house and couldn't even call her Vicki thought. He was no doubt embarrassed when he pulled up and seen her with Thomas, but going over to Shan house to get all in her business, he was doing too much Vicki thought. She got in the car and buckled up her seat belt. She thought about how James knew who Thomas was and that Vicki was messing with him, but Thomas knew nothing about James. Thomas would think James was a young punk. Her thoughts were snapped back to Thomas. "Was that Shan man Vicki?" She started looking through Thomas's C.D. collection. She didn't feel like answering him. "Yeah, I knew that ho wouldn't settle down with one nigga. That girl gets around. She like a fucking door knob everybody get a turn." He stared laughing at his own stupid joke. Thomas always talked about Shan. He couldn't stand her. "Oh, you ain't gone tell me not to talk about your friend?" Vicki shook her head no. "Some times you just gotta call a spade a spade." Vicki couldn't concentrate on lunch or the conversation she was having with Thomas. She kept thinking about Eric. Thomas could tell something was bothering her. "What you thinking about Vicki is there something you need? What's on your mind?" She had to think of something fast. "No, nothing just stressing about school, you know it's my last semester. She knew he fully supported her going to school, he even purchased her books for her a couple of semesters. They were sipping the last of their ice tea when Vicki's pager went off. It was Eric, and Vicki had to fight to suppress her smile. "Thomas I need to go use the phone." She stood up. "Who is it? You can use my cell phone." She shook her head no. "That's okay, it's my mother, I'll just use the pay phone." He twisted his lips at her like he didn't believe her then he blew her a kiss. She had to stop herself from running to the phone. When he answered the phone she closed her eyes. He sounded so good. "Hey Eric it's Vicki". "Hey pretty lady, you called me earlier? I told you I had a meeting." She was smiling the whole time. "I know but a girl can dream." He started laughing. "Listen, I'm going out of town tomorrow morning, I leave at six in the morning. So come over here and spent the night with me. I'll leave you money to catch a taxi home." "Okay, I'd love to." "Where are you now?" "I'm at lunch with a friend of mine." "Is it James?" Vicki smiled, she felt flattered that Eric remembered James, and was trying to sound jealous. "No, it's a girlfriend from school." "Oh, well in that case tell her to drop you off over here, I'll give her gas money for the drive. I'll be waiting on you." They hung up. Vicki wondered how she was going to get out of spending the rest of the day with Thomas. How was she going to tell him she had to cut the day short? When she got back to the table it just came out. "I have to go." Thomas looked at her like she was crazy. "Is everything okay Vicki?" Vicki took hold of Thomas's concern and decided to play it out. "Uh well, I just need to go, I'll talk to you about it later." They left the restaurant and rode home in silence, she felt bad for doing Thomas this way, but her man had to come first. She couldn't tell Thomas about Eric. He wouldn't have it, and well she didn't want to loose Thomas. When they pulled up in front of her house, she reached for the door. "Wait" Thomas called out to her. He gave her a card and kissed her on the lips. A tear ran down her face. He was so good to her. He wiped it off with his thumb "Don't worry Vicki, what ever it is you'll be fine. If you need me call me." She got out of the car and went into the house. She leaned against the door and was about to open the card when the phone rang. "Hello" It was Eric. Vicki, what happened, what are you doing at home?" She couldn't believe he was calling her again. He really wanted to see her. "Oh she couldn't bring me she had to pick up her daughter." The lies were coming fast and easy. "Yeah well I need to see you. I'm on my way to come and get you." "Okay see you soon." Vicki went to her room and placed the unopened card on her vanity set. Thoughts of Thomas quickly vanished. She packed her bag and filled her thoughts with Eric, and how wonderful he is.

CHAPTER 4

Eric lived in a small city across the Golden Gate Bridge. He always seemed astounded when he crossed that old orange bridge, like he was a tourist new to San Francisco. Vicki never paid it any mind. It was just another one of the many bridges in the Bay Area. To get from one city to the next. Twenty minutes after Eric had called; Vicki was outside checking the mail. Eric was pulling up in her driveway. She started grinning like a schoolgirl. "Wow Eric, that was fast. How did you get here so fast?" "Yeah I know, I was anxious to see my girl, is that a crime? Now come on let's get out of here." She made a mad dash to her room to get her over night bag. As she was coming out of the house she saw Shan and James getting into his car. The car pulled off, but not before she heard Shan speak to Eric, and start laughing. She went and got into the car with Eric. Eric asked her, "that was your friend Shan right, was that her man?" Eric obviously didn't remember James, and just because they were together why did everyone assume James was her man. She answered him without looking at him. "Yeah that was her, but that wasn't her man, just a friend."

He started the car and backed out of the driveway. "Why didn't you say something to her, we could have all went out and grabbed a bite to eat or something." She ignored him. She just turned her body sideways and focused her eyes out of the passenger side window. She closed her eyes and pretended to be sleep. She couldn't stop thinking about Shan and James. She kind of understood why Shan wasn't speaking to her, but James she couldn't understand. Shan was probably filling his head with lies and shit about her she thought. Just like Shan to player hate on her.

When they got upstairs it was of box of chocolates on the counter. She turned to face Eric after she noticed it. "Sweets for my sweetie." He said as he took her in his arms. He could feel that she was a little tense. "Don't worry Vicki, what ever is going on with you and your friend you will get past it. If you are truly friends." She smiled up at him and rested her head on his chest. He was always so caring and concerned, and knew her so well she thought. "I uh, have to go out and pick up some take out. There is no food here. While I am out I'll pick up some movies, go ahead and rest I'll be back shortly." "No Eric, I'll go with you I don't want to rest." He put his hand up to protest then rubbed it over his hair. He was always smoothing down his hair. Eric had what black folks called good hair. "No, besides I need to stop by the office and pick up some files for my trip. He kissed her on the forehead and was out the door. He had told her that their relationship was their business. That for professional reasons they would keep it out of both offices. She went into his bedroom to lay down. She wasn't tired but she did have a lot on her mind. Shan, James, Thomas, and plus school was getting ready to start. His suitcase was on the bed. She tried to fasten it so she could move it to the floor, but it was too full. She smiled to herself as she thought of how much he needed a good woman in his life. He can't even pack a suitcase. She started rearranging the clothes in the suitcase. She noticed some baby clothes in the bottom under his T-shirts and boxers. Vicki was baffled. Eric never told her he had a baby. There weren't any pictures of any babies around the apartment. She decided to look around the apartment and she what she could find. Ordinarily she would not do this, but she had a strange feeling. She found his airline ticket in the nightstand drawer, it read Eric Matthews. Her heart started to beat a little faster. She threw it on the bed next to the suitcase. She opened the walk in closet and turned the light on. She started going through boxes on the shelves and emptying out the drawers. On the top shelf in the back she felt a picture frame. She pulled the picture out of the shelf. It was an eight by ten of one of the most beautiful women she had ever seen. She had the perfect skin tone, like a reddish brown color. Her eyes were shaped like almonds and she had curly hair that hung down her back. She had a smile on her face and her head tilted back in a way that made her look, innocent and seductive. Vicki threw the picture across the room and it crashed into the wall shattering the glass. She picked up the suitcase and emptied the contents all over the room. She wanted to do more. She picked up the airline ticket and ripped it up. She thought about searching the apartment to see what else she could find, but she decided the best thing was to just get the hell out. She called Shan. She had to swallow her pride and get back across that bridge. She called her house to see if Vernon was there but no answer. She called a taxi. She had it pick her up from the coffee shop up the block. She didn't want to be in that apartment when Eric came back. When she arrived across the bridge she noticed that the meter already read $24.47. All she had was twenty-five dollars in cash. She told the driver to pull over. She gave him the twenty-five dollars and got out of the cab. Before she closed the door she heard the driver say, "Hey lady, thanks for the tip big spender." She looked back up at the meter and it had moved up to twenty-four dollars and eighty-seven cents. She cut her eyes at him and flipped him off. He sped off. She walked around ten blocks and it felt like ten country miles. She wasn't sure what she was going to do. She called her old faithful stand by, collect. It was after five o'clock and she didn't know what she was going to tell Thomas after running out on him earlier without explanation, and having him drop her off at home. Now here she was on the other side of town with swollen red eyes and an overnight bag. She tried to come up with something as she stood on the side of the phone booth waiting for Thomas. He pulled up and she got in. He rubbed her hand then put his back on the wheel and they rode to his house in silence.

Thomas didn't ask Vicki any questions. He had plenty but he was just happy to be with her, and he didn't want to create any friction. After Vicki relaxed they played a few games of dominoes, ordered a pizza and watched a movie. "Thomas, don't you have any other movies besides these old guns, blood, and shoot em up?" He looked at her and she knew that was a stupid question. Before the movie got started good Vicki was sleep. Thomas just watched her. He wanted her so bad. Maybe he was too nice to her. She deserved it though. She was trying to do something with herself instead of waiting on some man to take care of her. He caressed the side of her face with the back of his had until he as also sleep. When Vicki opened her eyes, she looked over at Thomas. He was sleeping so soundly. She looked over on his nightstand and there was enough jewelry and cash to feed a small country. She shook her head. If only he was legit. She might of thought about getting serious with him, but all the shady things he was in to. Always looking over his shoulder and acting paranoid like someone was out to get him. That was just too much drama for her Vicki thought. It made her nervous sometimes being out with him. She decided to go ahead and get ready for bed. She got her bag and headed for the bathroom to take a shower. When she got out of the shower, she was looking in her bag for hear nightshirt and noticed her pager had been going off. It had four pages on it. The first one was from Vernon. She told herself she would call him first thing in the morning. The other three were from Eric he was paging her putting 911 indicating that it was an emergency. She started to cry silently as she slid down to the bathroom floor. She wanted to call him and that made her more sad. Didn't she deserve some sort of explanation? Maybe she was jumping to conclusions. She turned the pager off and put it back in the bag. She walked out and headed for the phone in the kitchen. As she walked past the bedroom, she noticed Thomas. He looked so handsome in his black FUBU jeans and no shirt. She leaned up against the doorframe and imagined waking up to Thomas everyday. Surprisingly that gave her a warm feeling. She smiled to herself and walked over and climbed on top of him. She started kissing him very softly on his face and his neck. He didn't open his eyes, but Vicki knew he was wake. She could feel him getting hard. He started to caress her body. She kissed him on the lips and opened his mouth with her tongue. His breath was hot but he tasted good and she was really enjoying kissing him. He opened his eyes and held her at the shoulders and looked her in the eyes. "You don't have to do this, you know I am here for you no matter what Vicki, no strings." She picked up the remote to the television and turned it off. She pulled her gown over her head and exposed her breast. She took him by the wrist and guided his hands to her breast. He began to massage them. She let out a low groan. She leaned forward and kissed him. He placed one her nipples in his mouth and fondled the other. Thomas undid his pants and got a condom from his nightstand. He put it on while Vicki continued to kiss him all over his body. He lifted her slightly and placed himself gently inside her. Thomas was making her feel so good. She wanted to make sure he was getting as much out of this as she was. She started bucking like a horse while Thomas had a hold of her hips. He was moaning and calling her name. That encouraged her and she started twirling her hips around and thrusting her pelvis against him. She exploded form the inside and fell against his chest. He flipped her over on to her back and spread her legs; he gave a few quick thrusts and began to shake. After a few minutes he caught his breath and pulled himself out. He took the condom off wrapped it in a tissue and threw it in the wastebasket next to his bed. He held Vicki from behind and they fell asleep in that embrace. Vicki thought about Eric, and how he never made her feel this good. Thomas thought about Vicki, she was so erratic, he never knew what to expect with her. He didn't want to let her go. He wasn't' going to get ahead of himself.

CHAPTER 5

The next week Vicki spent every day with Thomas. She was fully aware that he was just a crutch helping her deal with what ever happened with Eric. She was bothered that he hadn't tried to contact her while he was out of town. She figured she would just have to stay busy and wait to run into him when he got back into town. She would eventually have to see him.

No luck running into him. He was back in town and two weeks had passed. No errands needed to be run over to Jacobs and Sons. Vicki finally started to except that she had lost him. Without him even asking for a chance to explain. He didn't even give her a chance to take him back. That pissed her off. She began to isolate herself from everyone. Thomas, Vernon her mother, and even her co-workers. On her last day, she cleared out a few things and was preparing to leave. She called Thomas and told him not to pick her up that she was staying late for a going away party and she would call him later. She knew she wouldn't, she wanted to get some alcohol, lock herself in her room and drink herself to sleep. Besides Monday school was starting and she needed to just stay home this weekend. She needed to prepare herself mentally for her last semester. She would still work, but only on Mondays and Fridays. That was enough for her. She was sick of these folks anyway. When she walked out of her building Eric was standing there leaning against his car. She stopped dead in her tracks. She felt like if she were to take a step she would collapse. Over a month had passed, and here he was just popping up and had the nerve to still be looking good. She took a deep breath and let it out slowly. She bit her bottom lip. "Victoria, we need to talk, this has gone on long enough. I'm not just going to let you walk out of my life. I need you. Now I gave you enough time to calm down after your little temper tantrum at the apartment." She couldn't believe her ears. Did Eric just say he needed her? Damn he was fine. She wasn't about to give in that easily. He hurt her bad and then left her to her own thoughts. To assume the worse. He walked over to her and tried to take the box from her arms, she resisted him. She missed him, but hell he left her hanging and she wasn't about to just pick up where they left off. "Eric look, it's been…" He cut her off. "No, listen, you haven't let me explain the situation. You deserve that much. If you choose not to see me after that fine." Fat chance she thought to herself. She didn't want to loose him by playing too hard. She stared at him coldly and handed him the box. He put it in his trunk. He opened the door for her and she got in. He ran around to the driver's side and got in. he looked at her real hard. "Damn I missed you Vicki, you look good, how was work?" "Eric spare me. However long it takes you to drive me home is how long you have to explain yourself. So just skip the pleasantries." She crossed her arms over her chest. "I shouldn't be in the car with a stranger any way." He started laughing. "That didn't stop you the night you met me." She jerked her head around in his direction. "Well I could just get out now you bastard." He started up the car and pulled off. "You ain't getting out, you know you don't want to and you know I don't want you to. I'll take you home, but since my time is limited, can you please listen?" He took a deep breath, cleared his throat, and ran his hand over his head. Vicki rolled her eyes and focused on the road. "My last name is Matthews, Eric Matthews. You assumed on your own that it was Jacobs."

She interrupted him. "What the hell else was I suppose to think, you just go around passing yourself off as…" He cut her off. "Let me finish before you start badgering me with questions. I never corrected you because it just never crossed my mind. Clifford, well Mr. Jacobs is my father; he's my father in law. That picture you found is his daughter. My wife." Vicki's chest started to hurt. She was breathing heavy. She had figured that much, but to hear Eric admit to it really hurt. "And the baby clothes, huh Eric, you have a brand new fucking baby." He swerved the car over to the curb and put it in park. "Watch your mouth, you suppose to be a lady and there is no need for that. I know you are hurt, but you need to calm down and listen." She was crying uncontrollably. She felt scared and nervous. She wanted to jump out of the car and run. He held her face and wiped here tears. She was beginning to calm down. He stared at her and then a tear ran down his cheek. "Vicki, please don't do this, don't leave me. I love you." She melted on the inside. Vicki felt like she left her own body. She loved him so much, and he loved her. They each leaned back in the seat and sat in silence holding hands until the sun went down. Vicki couldn't remember any of the conversation. She didn't care. She remembered Eric telling her he loves her and to give it some time, a little more time. He could have an eternity she thought, or at least the rest of her life.

CHAPTER 6

Three weeks into school and Vicki found herself typing her research paper in her underwear at Eric's computer. Although he hadn't giving her a detailed explanation, Vicki was back in his bed, his heart now. He loved her, and told her everyday. Mondays and Fridays they ate lunch together, then he dropped her off at work. It had become their routine. Thomas tried paging Vicki, and she paid him no mind. She and Shan started speaking again but now Shan was avoiding her. James was completely out of her life. A lot of times Vicki thought about James, but when the thoughts were to heavy and tears began to burn her eyes she filled her thoughts with Eric.

School had begun to get very hectic. It was Vicki's last semester and not only was she applying to graduate schools, she was trying to find a job. She would be getting her BA in Child Psychology in less than three months and she was very excited. Eric promised her something major for graduation. After receiving keys to his apartment, she couldn't think of anything that would please her more. Except maybe divorce papers and an engagement ring.

Monday when Vicki got off work, she went home to give her and Eric a little breathing room. When she got home her mother was laid out on the couch with a bottle of gin next to her. She didn't budge when Vicki came in. Vicki just stared at her mother. It couldn't be that bad she thought. She hadn't seen her mother for more than five minutes in three months. She just watched her sleep and thought about how close they use to be. Just then she heard a familiar car outside. She opened the door. It was James; not alone he was dropping Shan and her son off. Then he kissed Shan. Long and passionate, like he used to kiss her. She slammed the door hard enough for them to hear it. Her mother didn't budge. She went into her room and slammed the door. "That bitch" she screamed. Somebody was knocking at her door. "Go away" she yelled. The door opened slowly. "V, it's me what's up?" "Come in Vernon" Vicki missed Vernon, she missed their talks and their weekends going out and trips with Veronica. Vicki sat up on her bed and Vernon sat across from her. He sat backward in the gold chair that went to the gold and white vanity set. "What is up with mama Vern?" "She's been that way for the past few weeks"

Vernon began. Last month pops packed up and left, told her he wasn't coming back. I had to pull her off of him." Vicki was crying uncontrollably. "Why didn't anyone call me?" "I called your job at least four times, you were so busy you claimed. I paged you, you didn't callback. I couldn't hunt you down." Vicki thought of all the times she ignored Vernon's pages, and promises she made to call him back when he did call her at work. Vicki was hurt. Vernon was hurt to. His father had walked out on his mother, and his best friend, his sister had deserted him. He had to deal with his parents split, and his mothers pain on his own. Her drinking spells, passing out on the couch, she's lost her job. It wasn't easy for him. They sat there in silence for a few minutes, while Vicki let the news of her family falling apart sink in. Vernon broke the silence, and told Vicki she needed to take those braids out her hair. The image of Shan and James came into her head. "Vernon, what's going on with Shan and James?" Vernon stared at Vicki, he contemplated on telling her a lie, but she needed to know what was up. "Vicki, they been seeing each other for a while now, like I said you weren't talking to anyone, I assumed you knew and that's why you threw yourself at that brother Eric." Vicki felt a lump in her throat. She fought back her tears. "How long Vernon"? He could tell she was hurt, Shan was her best friend, and he knew how much she liked or used to like James and he didn't want to answer her. "How long Vern, Damn?" "Well I'm not sure, but the night y'all went out to that new club me and Brenda was pulling up and he was parked outside the house. He said he was waiting for you. So I let Brenda in and sat outside and waited for a minute. When Shan pulled up I thought you was with her so I went in. When I was bringing Brenda home in the morning he was just leaving. So draw yo' own conclusions. Look Vicki, you about to graduate, you got this new brother he seem to have it together, don't let them two get to you." He got up and walked out the door. "..and take them stale ass braids out yo' head" He closed the door just before she threw a pillow at him. She got up and pushed the lock in on her door. Vicki lay on her back and started crying silently as she took her braids out.

CHAPTER 7

Vicki had gotten a job offer at the Youth Guidance center to do counseling for young people incarcerated. She was scheduled to start six weeks after graduation. Her and Eric celebrated all nightlong and all day when she got the news. Monday after school Vicki met Thomas at the Chevy's restaurant up the street from her school. She told him about graduation, he told her about his promotion at work. He also told her she was the only woman he loved. Before she could respond he said, "I just wanted you to know that before I told you I'll be getting married in December". What the hell was going on? Vicki's head was spinning. Vicki got up and grabbed her purse. "Have a nice life Thomas." She walked out of the restaurant. She knew Thomas would let her go. She felt sad. She always thought she would always have a chance with Thomas, but now he was getting married. She caught the train downtown and went to work. She had a dozen roses with a card on her desk. "They came a few minutes ago" Lita said. "Are they from Eric or Thomas, maybe an apology from James?" Vicki always shared what was going on in her life with Lita.

The time she worked there, her and Lita had become pretty close. Vicki opened the card. It was from Eric. "Sorry we couldn't do lunch, meet me at the apartment. Love E".

When Vicki got to Eric's apartment there was a black teddy lying on his bed with a DKNY perfume set. Vicki showered with the shower gel and sprayed herself down. She repainted her toenails and put on the lingerie. She went to the kitchen and opened the fridge. There was another card. "He is so sweet," she said aloud. The card instructed her to set the table for a romantic night; "I need to lose myself in you". She read the words over and over. Vicki set the table as her man requested. It looked like a scene form a movie. Lace table cloth and sterling silver candle set. Two champagne glasses. Rose pedals around the table and black plates. Vicki folded red cloth napkins on the side of the plates. When she heard the key in the door she lit the candles and turned off the lights. She stood by the table under the flicker of the candlelight and Eric came in. He watched her with his green eyes and Vicki could feel her body responding from his sensual stare. Eric was carrying a paper bag. He had t.v. dinner's, not what she expected, but being with him would more than make up for it. She smiled to herself as she warmed them in the microwave and removed the dinners from the plastic trays and placed them on the plates. Eric showered and came out wearing a silk robe. It was tied around the waist revealing his muscular butt, but opened at the top showing off his six pack. They ate dinner over constant complements of Vicki. He loved her hair. He wondered why she even wore those braids. Her hair fell just on her shoulders. She wore a part in the middle and the hair fell straight down all the way around her head. It had been flat ironed and bumped under. When she walked or nodded her hair moved like silk. When Eric blew the candles out, Vicki got up from her chair. She pulled the table toward her. She straddled herself across Eric's lap facing him. Nothing separated their bodies from being one, but the silk robe he was wearing and the black teddy she was wearing. She untied his robe and he lifted her up and placed himself inside of her. She closed her eyes and rocked back and forth. She imagined riding on her favorite roller coaster.

That morning Eric went to work and Vicki stayed sleep. When she got out the bed around ten, she cleaned Eric's apartment careful not to stumble on any extra information. She was in love and so was he; it'll work itself out.

"SURPRISE" When Vicki walked in her mothers house their was a surprise party. For her…Family, friends, co-workers, classmates from college, and even high school. "Happy graduation baby." Her mother looked beautiful. She wore a soft pink dress with baby blue flowers on it. She had her hair pulled up in a bun, and she was smiling and crying at the same time. "Thank you mommy" Vicki hugged her mother, this was the lady that she was so close to. Right behind her was her father. "That's my girl, I knew you would make it." It's no wonder her mother looked so happy, he was here. Vicki smiled and went into her father's embrace. She looked over at her brother Vernon, not sure what to do or say next. Vernon pressed the play button on the c.d. player and a song from Tupac came blaring out the speakers. "Lets party" he yelled. Everyone began breaking off into different little cliques. Dancing, talking, eating, and drinking. Vicki was dancing with Vernon; she was having a good time. Brenda walked over and smiled at Vicki. They hugged and Vicki left Vernon to Brenda and she went to mingle. Vicki was coming out of the bathroom and James was standing right in front of the door. They stared at each other for what seemed like hours to Vicki. James leaned in to kiss Vicki; she wasn't going to resist him. "James" a voice called from the other end of the hall. They both jumped. It was Shan. James didn't turn around, he just looked Vicki in the eyes and told her they needed to talk. Before Vicki gave a response James walked up the hall. He brushed past Shan and disappeared into the crowd. Vicki started up the hall; she wasn't about to speak to Shan. "Victoria, you'll talk to James but not me, your best friend." Shan had tears in her eyes. It didn't move Vicki. "I am so proud of you Vicki, I am. I love you" Vicki started to soften up. "We'll talk later Shan". That was all Vicki could get out. Thomas was talking to Vernon when he spotted Vicki staring at him. He wiggled his index finger and motioned Vicki to come to him. Just then the music stopped. Her mother was yelling, "gift time, time to open the presents." Vicki sat in the chair next to a table stacked with gifts. She opened Vernon gift first. It was a blue and white Nike sweat suit, with matching tennis shoes. Then her mother's gift. The card read from mom and dad. It was a gold chain with a floating heart. The heart had a diamond in it. Vicki opened up the rest of her gifts. Thomas's gift was money; James had given her a gold bracelet. Shan gave her an orange sweater from the GAP. Vicki was about to start thanking everyone for coming and the gifts and Thomas interrupted her. "One more Vicki" he threw a small box across the room and Vicki caught it. Her heart started pounding. I can't be the one he thinks he's marrying she thought as she held the small box and her hand shook. I love Tommy, but I have Eric. Her brother interrupted her thoughts. "Open it damn" She unwrapped the gold wrapping carefully like a surgeon. The box didn't look like a ring box. Vicki felt relieved. She lifted the top and it was two keys on a ring. Vicki looked up suspiciously at Thomas. "It's yours," he said. "What's mine?" She asked in a shaky voice. "Look in the garage." She walked over to the kitchen and opened the door that led to the garage. It was the BMW. It was painted midnight blue, and it had personalized plates with her name.

Vicki started crying. "Thomas I can't" "I can, give me the keys," somebody said. Vicki didn't recognize the voice. She just walked over to Thomas and hugged him. Thomas was so good to her. He deserved to be happy she thought as he held her in his arms. The rest of the guest seem to vanish. She knew he loved her, but he was moving on with his life, getting married, and she was moving on with hers. Loving Eric. Thomas and Vicki would have to settle for memories, and friendship.

CHAPTER 8

Today was Vicki's first day of work. She was up much earlier than she needed to be. The building was only a fifteen-minute drive away from her house. She went to the kitchen and made herself some toast and spread with cream cheese. After she ate she decided to call Eric. He answered on the first ring and Vicki knew he was on the other line. He clicked over and left her on hold for at least five minutes. He came back to the line. "Hey Lady, how is my baby feeling on her first day of work?" Vicki wasn't letting him get off that easily. "Who were you on the phone with Eric?" He didn't answer her. He had a bad habit of not answering her when he felt like he didn't have to. That really pissed her off. Like once she asked him when he thought he would be filing for divorce. He ignored her like he didn't hear the question. Just kept on watching television. A few minutes later he started talking about something that was on television. So she just let it go, just like she was about to do now. "Sooo, are you nervous, excited, or what?" "I guess I am a combination of both. It all just sort of happened faster than I expected." "Well it's natural for you to feel nervous, just turn it into confidence, they knew what they were doing when they hired you baby." He always said the right things, he was so smart. "Thank you Eric, you always tell me what I need to hear." "What are you doing up so early, you got yourself a little BMW from your little thug drug dealing gangster boyfriend. You could drive to work, hopefully the police don't stop you for driving the car used in the last drive by." He started laughing like he just told the joke of the year on def-comedy jam. "He's not my boyfriend Eric, and you don't even know him to be making comments like…" He cut her off. "Vicki please, I am not stupid, and you don't know who I know. A niggah give my girl a punk ass car…" She cut him off. "You didn't give me nothing" As soon as she said it, she wished she could take it back. "Oh so it's like that. I didn't give you nothing, I didn't know you were a materialistic bitch, you on the phone early in the morning with me defending the next motherf…" She hung up the phone in his face. The word bitch hung in her head. She didn't feel like hearing Eric go on another one of his trips about friends she don't even see anymore when he has a wife and a child some where. All that cursing, sometimes she swore this man was Dr.Jeckel and Mr.Hyde. She wasn't going to let Eric ruin her first day of work. She'd just call him later and let him apologize.

Vicki changed her clothes at least four times. She settled on her black pants suit. She pulled up in the employee parking lot behind the building and was on her way. She felt good. She made her way to the sixth floor where her office was. Lord knows she knew her way around all the time her and her parents spent in the Youth guidance center behind Vernon. The door read Y.G.C. COUNCELING SERVICES. She opened the door and went into the tiny waiting room with four chairs. There was a round table in the middle of the room with out-dated magazines of home and garden and reader digest. She made a mental note to replace those with Ebony and Essence. She might even throw in Vogue, so no one would trip. In front of her door was the secretary's desk. Vicki hadn't met her yet. Vicki looked at her own name on the door behind the small desk. Someone coming in the door startled her. The lady smiled, "I'm Gloria Winters, you must be Ms.Dupree?" She extended her hand

and Vicki shook it. "No" Vicki said, Gloria looked puzzled. Vicki noticed the look on the woman's face and smiled. "Well yes, I am Ms. Dupree but please call me Vicki, May I call you Gloria?" Vicki felt strange being called Ms.Dupree that was her mother's name and besides Gloria looked a little bit older than her. "Yes of course, call me Gloria, I arranged a few things for your arrival, shall we?" She motioned towards the door that led to Vicki's office. It was small but she could work with it. It had a big leather chair that sat behind the desk a sofa up against the wall and a file cabinet in the corner. There were two chairs that sat in front of the desk. There was a plant on Vicki's desk. She looked over at Gloria. "Sort of a office warming for you Vicki, hope you like it." Vicki knew her and Gloria would get along well. "Yes, it's nice, thank you." Gloria walked over to the file cabinet and pulled out some files. She handed them to Vicki and told her they were files of the inmates she would be counseling her first quarter. "I'll leave you to go through them or get settled in, I'll be at my desk if you need anything" She smiled at Vicki. "Thank you for everything Gloria." She walked out and closed the door behind her.

Vicki started going over her files. There was one young man in particular that caught her eye. His name was TreVeon Spencer. He had been in the center since he was fourteen and would remain until his eighteenth birthday. What surprised her was that there was no crime. His detainment was a result of parent's request. She claimed she could not control him, and at most times feared him. At the young age of thirteen he shot his mothers boyfriend. After serving six months at a juvenile camp he came home. According to his mother he was drinking, smoking weed, staying out all hours of the night, and selling drugs from her home. She says when she questioned him about it he became irate, and violent. She asked the authorities to pick him up. At first he was placed several times in various group homes, but he kept either fighting or running away. He was then placed in Y.G.C. for constant supervision and counseling. Vicki felt bad for him. He was probably just miss-understood. She was going to pay extra attention to him.

All day and no word from Eric. Vicki had left him a message but he didn't return her call. At five o'clock Gloria buzzed Vicki and told her not to work too hard, and that she was leaving for the day. Vicki thought that was a good idea. The last thing she asked Gloria to do was make sure they had a new file cabinet delivered. She wanted to start her own files; she would just use the previous counselor's files as reference notes. Vicki went to her car pressed the alarm and got in. As she was pulling out she noticed she need gas. Thank goodness there was a gas station right next to her building. She pulled up to a pump and went in to pay for her gas. When she came out some man was at her car pumping her gas. Damn, she thought to herself, the bums just got bold don't even ask anymore. She started looking in her purse for a dollar or some change to give him. When she walked closer, she realized she knew the bum. He turned around smiling. He pulled his hat off his head and held it out like he was begging. "Pump you gas for a kwater ma'am". Vicki couldn't help but laugh. "Oh you begging now James Roberts?" They started laughing. "I was at the light and I saw you pull into the station. Let me take you to dinner so we could have that talk". Vicki wasn't sure if that was a good idea; there was still a small part in her heart that

James occupied. But, she was hungry, and it would be a free meal on James. "You sure your girl Shan won't mind?" Vicki had to throw that in his face. She went to the driver's side and got in. He finished pumping her gas and walked up to the window. She rolled it down. "I deserve that, but you sure yo' man that gave you this car wont mind, or the one with the red drop? You just got buck wild now little Vicki, and hung me out like wet laundry." She looked up at James. "First you know Thomas ain't my man, and the red drop, well that ain't cha' business. Now where are we going to eat?" He shook his head and smiled. "You sure have changed from the girl that was sprung on me since ninth grade. Meet me at McGees." He jogged over to his car, got in and peeled off. James was right she had changed she thought to herself. I grew up, and he didn't.

By the time Vicki got to McGees, James was already at a table with a drink in his hand. As she made her way to the table she had to laugh at how James always did drive like a bat out of hell. "I ordered you a kamikaze, no ice. I also ordered you the sautéed shrimp, wild rice and steamed broccoli." He looked pleased with himself. "You remembered, you can be a sweetheart and not always a cheating jerk." James took a sip from his drink. "Look Vicki, I'm sorry. It wasn't suppose to go down like it did, but now we had that kind of relationship". He sipped his drink again, he knew that wasn't a good enough excuse for Vicki, she was too smart. "Yeah because you kept me holding on waiting for a commitment, and that is beside the point, Shan was my best friend. You didn't have to push up on her." James wrinkled his forehead. "Look I don't know what you heard, but she pushed up on me. When she pulled up that night you went home with the next nigga, I thought you were in the car with her. I got out and went over to the car and she told me you went home with dude and you weren't tripping off of me. She told me to come upstairs she was about to fry some chicken and she had some bomb weed. We fired up the joint had a few more drinks and yo' girl was all over me." Vicki didn't know what to think. "Well I called her, she didn't say you were in her apartment, she said…" He cut her off. "I know what she said, she said James is parked outside you house, then she asked you something about if I was yo man. I was sitting right there.

She was telling me to be quiet". Vicki swallowed hard. She was past this Shan and James thing. She always knew how Shan was, they say best friends are the ones to stab you in the front. Vicki and James ate dinner and talked about her new job and her family. They had another round of drinks and the next thing Vicki knew she was following James to a hotel. They got a room and were tearing each other's clothes off before the door closed. He is such a dog she kept telling herself. Why am I even here? She kept asking herself. Her head kept telling her to stop and get the hell out of there, but James felt so good grinding up against her and kissing her with so much force. James and Vicki had chemistry. They didn't really make love, it was more raw sex, but damn if it didn't feel good to Vicki she thought to herself as they tore each other's clothes off. After they finished, they laid next to each other on the floor stark naked and out of breath. James took off the condom he didn't want to wear and threw it across the room. He let out a howl. That use to make Vicki laugh. Now it disgusted her. "I know you man can't break you off like that." He gave her a quick kiss on the cheek and went into the bathroom. Vicki felt sick to her stomach. She couldn't believe what she had just done. She got dressed in a hurry while James was in the shower, and left the room. When she got home she jumped in the shower. As the steaming hot water beat down on her body she prayed to God through tears to forgive her and bless her. She prepared herself for work the next day. She checked her parent's room. She wanted to talk to her mother, but she was already sleep. Her father wasn't there, and Vernon was gone to work. She felt so alone. She closed her room door, got in her bed and cried herself to sleep.

The whole week had passed and Vicki hadn't heard from Eric. It was eating her up on the inside. She refused to call him. He owed her the apology not the other way around. She did have some pride. Here it was now Friday and she was stuck at home. Vernon came in and asked her if she wanted to go bowling with him and Brenda. She declined that offer. She thought about calling James, but he was so pissed off at her for leaving the room like she did, she changed her mind. She would just have to hang with herself this Friday night. Monday was her first appointment with two of her counsels. On of them was TreVeon Spencer. She went to her office and started outlining her sessions.

The weekend came and went. Saturday all Vicki did was go grocery shopping with her mother. Sunday her mother dragged her to church. Told her as long as her soul was troubled her life would be troubled. Once she got past the stares and whispers she enjoyed the services. Going to church always made her feel humble. Where her mother was a member the entire congregation sang and they sang in A cappella. No piano drums not even a tambourine. It filled her spirit and she felt good. Just her luck the sermon was on fornication and she swore the whole time the minister wanted to call her by name. She hadn't been to church in a long time, and it was something she needed to start thinking about.

Monday she went to work early to prepare for her sessions. Her ten o'clock was with TreVeon. She went over his case file over and over again. Gloria came in at nine as usual. She was always so happy Vicki thought. "Hey Gloria" Vicki liked her and they were becoming close. They had went to lunch together twice last week, even went shopping together. Vicki helped Gloria pick out a bracelet for her man. The phone was ringing and Gloria answered it. "Oh hi, yes, no I'll be down at around 9:45, okay, love you" Vicki listened in on Gloria's conversation. She wanted her man to call her at work. In the words of Toni Braxton it had been seven whole days. Her thoughts were interrupted by Gloria's voice. "I need to run down stairs for a minute, you want a bagel?" "No thank you, take your time, just be back to warn me when my ten o'clock is here." Gloria strolled back in the office at 9:55 singing all the man I need. "You must be in love Ms. Gloria Winters?" Gloria laughed at how giddy she was being. "Yeah, my baby just stopped by. He is so sweet. I can't wait for you two to meet. His name is Avery and he treats me like a queen girl. We are having an engagement party in November. I would love for you to come." "I'll be there, I wouldn't miss it". Just as Vicki finished her sentence a deliveryman came in the office carrying a vase with red and pink roses. Gloria started smiling and Vicki turned her back to walk into her office. "Victoria Dupree?" Vicki stopped in her tracks. She turned around. "Are you sure?" "Are you Victoria Dupree?" "Yes but…" "Well sign here." He gave a clipboard to sign on and then handed her the vase and headed for the door. "Wait, let me tip you please." He held his hand up in protest. "It's already been covered". He turned and left. "Well Vicki, looks like I'm not the only one." Gloria said. Vicki carried the vase into her office and read the note. They were from Eric. The note read "Meet me at the apartment at eight O'clock. I am truly sorry, and I miss you. E" She almost cried.

At ten o'clock Gloria was buzzing Vicki's phone. "They're here Ms. Dupree." Vicki's heart started pounding she was expecting a monster to walk through the door. In walked this innocent looking kid no more than five feet tall. He was so black, he was almost blue, and he had the smoothest skin Vickie had ever seen. He had the nerve to have light brown eyes, and long thick curly eyelashes that any woman would kill for. He looked like an angel. Vicki just stood and stared at him for a few seconds. He looked like he blinked in slow motion. He winked one of his eyes at her and that snapped her back to attention. That is when she noticed he was in handcuffs and shackles. He was with a white man in a pair of worn out blue jeans and a raggedy Dallas Cowboy T-shirt. "Victoria, I'm Tony Spoons, TreVeon's probation officer. He thinks he is a charmer so watch out and good luck." Vicki looked over to TreVeon and the expression on his face had not changed. "Thank you Mr. Spoons, the session will be over in exactly one hour." She looked at her watch. "So before we get behind schedule, why don't you take the cuffs and ankle bracelets off so we can get started." "Not going to happen, Mr. Spencer here is high risk. He's tried running before. The cuffs stay on." She smiled at him without showing any teeth. "Please Mr.Spoons, I am sure he'll be fine. I feel more comfortable with him out of the cuffs. And since this is my time with him, I'll ask you again to please remove them." He blew out an agitated breath and took the cuffs and shackles off. TreVeon started rubbing his wrist. "Now he is in your custody, so if he takes off it's on you, even though you won't be the one hunting him down in the projects." Again she gave him the smile that revealed no teeth. "That will be all Mr.Spoons." He looked at TreVeon with an evil look and walked out of the room. TreVeon just stood there and stared at Vicki. She didn't know what to expect, but she had hoped for a bit of gratitude. She started to wonder what if he did make a run for it. Would she chase him, could she catch him, and if she did what the hell would he do? She smiled at him. "Have a seat Mr. Spencer, let's talk, just get to know one another." He let out a long sigh and sat down. Damn, this little niggah got attitude, Vicki thought. He started picking at his nails. She cleared her throat. "I'm Ms.Dupree, or Vicki which ever you prefer." He rolled his eyes. "I don't prefer shit, cuz it don't matter what I say, or prefer, you ain't no different than the rest of the phony mother fucka's up here, So just scribble down what ever the hell you want in my file and let me get back to the hall where I could finish shooting hoops. Shit, disturbing my game fort this bull shit. I don't need no damn counseling from no uptight old ass telling how the fuck I should behave. I'm here until I am eighteen so what difference does all this make? Damn" Vicki was floored. She was hardly prepared for this. Who the hell did this little punk ass boy think he was talking to like that? She wanted to tell him to watch his mouth, he didn't know who was talking to like that. But she thought better of it. "Look, I am not sure what you are use to, but I don't appreciate or tolerate that language. So please, respect me as an adult, as your counselor, and as a lady. You should always respect yourself, and further more, what you prefer does indeed matter. What Mr. Strack has here is old news. I will be starting a new file. We will start fresh. So let's not get off on the wrong foot. I want to help you but we have to get along." He started laughing. "Can't we all just get along" he mimicked the phrase made popular by Rodney King. "What you Rodney sister." Vicki wanted to laugh; she had to admit that was pretty funny. She had to remain professional. This boy was shooting her outline she spent so much time on to hell. She thought about how hard Vernon use to be growing up, how hard he still is. She changed her approach. "Look, we both have to be here. You, well its part of your sentence to have continuous counseling, and me, well I gots to get paid." He started laughing. "What is so funny?" Vicki asked him through a curious half of a smile. "Who taught you how to talk like that, you gots to get paid." What you watched some rap videos or something before this meeting so you can try and relate to me?" "What, how old do you think I am Mr. Spencer?" He put his index finger on his left temple and closed his eyes like he was thinking real hard. "Well with this job, and you must have kids about my age..." I don't mean to cut you off, but I don't have any kids, especially not your age." "Al'ite, you at least thirty, thirty five." Now Vicki was the one laughing.

For the rest of the session Vicki got him to open up simply by being his friend. Something she was sure Mr. Strack never tried. She told him who the roses were from, he told her abut the time he picked his mother some roses and she whipped him for being in someone else yard. Vicki also learned he was an only child, and that his mother had been addicted to crack and never paid him any mind. He did all kinds of things to get her love and attention. Including shooting a man that was beating her almost every night. At eleven o'clock Gloria buzzed Vicki. "Vicki are you okay, the session is over." "Yes Gloria, everything is fine, send Mr. Spoons in when he arrives." He sucked his teeth. "That bitch don't like me." Vicki shook her head at him. Don't call her that. She cool peoples." He started laughing. "Cool peoples, next time say cool peeps." They were laughing when Mr. Spoons came in and Vicki watched the smile fade from his face. "You still here kid." He started laughing as he put the chains and cuffs back on TreVeon. They turned to leave. Vicki called out to TreVeon. He turned around. "See you next week." He winked his eye at her and in a flash they were gone. Vicki put Mr. Stracks file in the old file cabinet. She was going to start her own file on TreVeon Spencer. She wanted to make a difference in his life.

At eight o'clock she was knocking at Eric's door. There was no answer. She was looking in her purse for a pen to leave a note and noticed her keys that he had given her. She let herself in and there was a note on the CD player that read "press play". She had already forgiven him when she got he roses. He was always thinking of something. She pressed play and Keith Sweat came blaring out of the speakers singing make it last forever. She loved Eric so much it hurt. She was going to make it last, even if it killed her. Dealing with Eric funny style ways was part of her now. She just needed to give him more time to fix his situation.

CHAPTER 9

November 13 was the day of Gloria's engagement party. Vicki was going to finally meet the wonderful Avery. She had to literally beg Eric to go with her. At first he flat out refused. Said he didn't give a damn about nobody engagement he didn't know. Vicki argued that Gloria was her friend and he could make an effort to get to know her friends. Or at least support her. "She ain't yo' friend Vicki, she's your damn secretary." After that remark she called to invite Thomas, but his number was changed. She finally convinced Vernon to go with her. After finding a baby sitter for Veronica and buying a new outfit all courtesy of Vicki's checking account, Vernon agreed to go. The morning of the party Eric changed his mind. Vernon didn't mind. He just laughed at Vicki and said since he had a baby sitter for the night and a new fit, he was going out with his boys. Vicki wore a red silk dress with thin straps that came just above her knees. She shaved and oiled her legs and wore her open toe red sandals. She pulled her hair up in a swoop bun in the back and straight bangs that fell to the left side. Eric wore black slacks, and a black shirt and his red Armani blazer.

Damn he was fine Vicki though as he stood in the mirror adjusting his collar. Vicki couldn't help feeling proud to be with him, they looked good together.

The evening was off to a bad start. First Vicki had to hear Eric complain about how she took too long with her make up. Then, an argument over which car to take. Vicki knew he was trying to stay home. But she wasn't going to let him off the hook. He never rode in her car any ways so she didn't even know why he tried dragging that dead horse up to beat. On the way to the hotel he didn't speak a word to her. Usually she would have just told him to take her home, but she promised Gloria she was coming. She just ignored him and kept checking her hair and makeup. He had to stop at the bank, stop and get gas, stop at the office. He was really pissing her off. She wanted to slap him in the back of the head. While he was in the office she called to see if Vernon was still home. She just as well went with him. He laughed at her and told her to deal with it, or just go by herself. I ain't your stand by, you better call Thomas with all that." He laughed and hung up on her. It was suppose to be a sit down dinner to start, then they were going to party in room Gloria reserved for dancing and drinking. Finally at the hotel, the valet took the keys. "Hey nice car man, nice woman too." "Yeah well if you scratch my woman, we'll have to talk, but if you scratch my car it's ya' ass." Eric started laughing and grabbed Vicki's hand. The guy looked at Vicki to get her reaction, and then he quickly averted his eyes. She just looked at Eric and rolled her eyes. When they got into the hall the dinner was over. Vicki was starving. The deejay was playing the latest cut from Nelly a rapper from the St.Louis area. "Damn Vicki we missed dinner, that's all I came for." Vicki rolled her eyes to the sky. Eric didn't want to be here and he was making it so hard on her. "Look Eric, you could just go home, and I'll catch a taxi." He walked away from her. A song by Vicki's favorite rapper LL.COOL J came on and she tried to loosen up. She took a step to walk around when she noticed Thomas. He was headed right in her direction. She hadn't talked to him since her gradation party. He stopped at a group of three women and a man. She tried to guess which one was the one he was going to marry. She snapped back into the party when Gloria caught her of guard. "Vicki you made it." They hugged each other tightly like good friends. Gloria looked great. She was wearing a black suede dress and black suede pumps. She had her hair pulled up, and was wearing some diamond studs in her ear. Nothing sparkled more than the two-carrot rock she had on her left hand. "Gloria, how are you lugging rock around, must be heavy girl." Gloria started squealing. "I just got it tonight, isn't it fabulous?" "It's beautiful girl." Vicki felt a bit of envy; she wanted to kick herself. Gloria deserved to be happy. Even if she wasn't. "Vicki, I want you to meet Avery, he's the most handsome man in the room." Vicki wished she had her handsome man by her side. "Where is Eric Vicki?" Before she could answer she noticed Thomas who noticed her at he same time. He was smiling at first but when he seen her the smile fell from his lips. She knew he was mad at her. "Hello earth to Vicki. Is something wrong Vicki, you want to step outside and talk?" Vicki cleared her throat. "No, I was uh, just wondering where Eric was." He walked up behind her. "I'm right here baby, how are you, I see with that diamond on your hand and glow on your face you must be Gloria, nice to meet you." Eric stepped from behind Vicki and gave Gloria a kiss on the cheek. He was so phony Vicki thought. "Nice to meet you too Eric, I've heard a lot about you." "Well it's not all true." They started laughing. Vicki had to remind herself to laugh. She was staring at Thomas so hard she didn't even know what was funny. Gloria turned to see what had Vicki's attention. "Avery" she called out. Gloria calling out to her fiancée interrupted Vicki's thoughts. Thomas started walking towards them. The smile on Gloria's face got bigger. What the hell is going on Vicki thought to herself. She started to feel dizzy. Why was Thomas on his way over here? Didn't he see Eric right behind her with his arms around her waist? She knew Thomas would not make a scene. When he got close to them Gloria put her arm around Thomas. "Hi baby" Vicki started shaking. Eric thought she was cold. He started rubbing her arms. She wanted to push is stupid ass acting like they were so happy when they weren't even speaking. "Vicki, this is my fiancée Avery." Vicki didn't move. Eric stepped from behind her and extended his hand to Thomas. "How are you, I'm Eric" There was obvious friction and tension in that introduction and hand shake. Avery this is

Vicki, my boss, and one of my bridesmaids if she excepts." Vicki's head started spinning. No this woman did not just ask her to be in her wedding, and why was she hugging Thomas and calling him Avery. "Oh, a Gloria, I don't know, I am sure you have friends you have known way longer than me." Gloria shook her head. "I consider you a good friend Vicki, time doesn't determine a friendship. Maybe it will put a fire under Eric." Vicki had the strangest look on her face. She thought she was going to throw up right on Gloria's suede shoes. Eric looked concerned. "Vicki are you okay?" No she wasn't okay, hell no. "I, a," She swallowed. "I don't really feel well. I think we should leave." "Oh Vicki are you going to be okay." Gloria asked her with real concern. "I'll be fine Gloria, I just need to go home." Eric put his blazer around Vicki. "Let's go baby, let daddy take care of you." Thomas dropped his glass. Gloria jumped back. "Are you and Vicki coming down with the same thing?" She started feeling his head. Then she hugged him.

Vicki and Eric left the party. Vicki told Eric to drop her off at her mother's house. He wanted to act like nothing was wrong with their relationship. After seeing how happy Gloria was Vicki didn't feel like pretending with Eric tonight. He damn sure wasn't getting any. She wanted to be that happy. Damn she cursed herself. That could have been her glowing and draped in diamonds with Thomas on her side. Instead she was shacking up with a married man who she had no idea when he was going to get a divorce. She was just going to except it. When they pulled up in front of her mother's house she took off the blazer and reach for the door handle. "Vicki wait, I know seeing Gloria and Avery tonight made you feel uncomfortable. I knew this would happen that is why I didn't want to go. I swear to you I love you and we will work this out, and be together. We'll be twice as happy as they could only dream of honey. Just give it some time." He stared her down with those eyes she fell in love with. A tear dropped from his eye. She wiped it off, and kissed him on the lips. "I know Eric, that you love me, but how much longer do you expect me to wait?" He looked down. She let out a sigh and got out of the car and closed the door. Eric sat in her driveway for what seemed like hours. Thinking about his life. "Damn, he said as he drove off, she does deserve better, but as long as she'll have me."

CHAPTER 10

It was two weeks before Christmas and three weeks before Thomas and Gloria's wedding. Vicki said her and Eric would be out of town for New Year's, so she couldn't be in her wedding. They really had no plans at all. Since they had been getting along so well Vicki decided not to push the issue when he totally ignored her questioning him about what they would be doing. At work Vicki began avoiding Gloria. She declined all invitations to lunch, or shopping after work and always worked with her door closed. Every time Gloria asked Vicki if something was wrong she just blamed it on some trouble with one of her counsels or Eric. Actually all of her sessions were going well. TreVeon was really opening up to Vicki. She was able to see that he was just a scared kid who needed someone to love and care for him. He needed and wanted to feel wanted.

Friday when Vicki got off work she went to the apartment. Eric was in the bedroom and started packing. "Where are you going Eric?" Eric looked up at Vicki with those eyes that use to melt her heart. Now they were just evil eyes she couldn't trust. "Victoria we need to talk, sit down." She dropped her purse and briefcase on the floor and sat on the bed with her hands folded in her lap. She knew it was news she didn't want to hear. He called her Victoria, that meant it was serious. She bit her bottom lip. "Look Victoria, Naomi wants me home for Christmas to spend with my daughter. So far she's been cool about me staying California, but I need to bend a little bit for her to keep calm." Vicki didn't say anything. What good would it do anyway? Why wouldn't a woman want her husband home for Christmas with her and her child? She just sat there and started to cry silently. "Vicki please, don't cry." He sat by her and she stood up. "Eric does she know about me?" He rubbed his hand over his hair and Vicki knew he was about to lie. "She knows I am seeing someone. She doesn't know how close we are or that I am seconds way from divorcing her. She does know that I don't love her any more or want to be with her. So she is using her father and my daughter to make sure I don't leave her. I swear, stick by me through this, as soon as I find another job I am leaving her." "Eric have you applied anywhere, what about Wrigler-Bryant, I mean have you been looking at all Eric?" He shook his head. "You know they won't hire me there, and yes I've been looking. I need to be hired on the senior level I am on. I've been in contact with several headhunters, but no one is willing to pay me what I am worth. I know I keep saying this but we just need time." He stood up and continued packing. She started helping him. She wasn't going to keep waiting on Eric. She was going to force him to make a decision at the first of the year.

Vicki spent the rest of the week in the apartment. Gloria called once and Vicki just promised to call her back. Shan called but they didn't talk very long. They were speaking yeah, and Shan was making every effort to mend the friendship they once had, but Vicki just couldn't let go. Shan took James from Vicki, as much as he was Vicki's. Vicki slept with James to spite Shan, it was just all too messed up. Vicki didn't want to deal with it. Gloria was more of a friend than Shan had ever been. She was right; time didn't determine a friendship. She decided to call Gloria back. Open up to her. Tell her that she dated Thomas in the past and it was a bit uncomfortable. No need to go into any details. Vicki called Gloria and Thomas answered the phone. Vicki hung up. She unplugged the phone. In the event he used the call return she didn't want the machine to pick up. She made her a sandwich and put on one of her favorite movies. *Waiting to Exhale.* After the movie was over she plugged the phone in, just in case Eric tried to call. He hadn't called all week, didn't even leave her a Christmas gift. Christmas was less than a week away and she hadn't even heard from him. She was looking through the movies and the phone rang. She just stared at it. The machine picked up. After the beep Eric came on. "Vicki, it's me..." She snatched up the phone. "Hi, hi Eric. I miss you." "Hey baby, why you screening the calls, you hiding from you trifling friend Shan." Vicki told Eric what Shan had done with James. "No, I just didn't reach the phone in time. I just walked in." "Oh, well I called earlier and the machine didn't pick up." Before she could think up a lie he started talking. "I miss you so much Vicki. I am just miserable here." Vicki took a deep breath. She missed him too. "I wish you were here Eric, I..." the line beeped. "Go ahead, it's probably your mother. I called there looking for you."

"Okay, well when will you call again?" The line beeped again. He ignored her. "Go ahead, I'll talk to you soon." He was gone. "Hello" Victoria this is Thomas. Don't hang up." Her heart pounded so hard she could hear it and feel it thumping against her chest. "Look, you don't have to say anything, just meet me at the Cozy Inn in twenty minutes." He hung up. Vicki sat on the couch with the phone in her lap for at least twenty minutes. Thomas, Avery, Thomas Avery, Avery Thomas, Thomas Avery Jones. Vicki never even knew Thomas had a middle name. Let alone it would be Avery. She decided to go. Put some closure to this so she could get on with her working relationship and friendship with Gloria. When she got into the car she cried. Thomas had told her time and time again he wanted to be with her, and now he was taken and happy. She was miserable. She took him for granted. Chose James over him, then Eric. What a damn fool she thought.

When she got to the bar, Thomas was sitting in the corner checking his watch. He looked better than she ever remembered him. His dark skin looked extra smooth. Gloria must be taking good care of him she thought. He sported a goatee, and it looked extra neat and well trimmed. He sported a low cut fade with a part on the side. He had two earrings in his left ear. One loop and one diamond, and one loop in his right ear. Vicki always did go for that thug appeal. When he looked up and seen Vicki staring at him, he stood up. He crossed his hands in front of his crouch. Vicki noticed the bracelet that she helped Gloria pick out. Gloria had told Vicki that he loved it. She had no idea the whole time Gloria was talking about Thomas. All six feet two inches two hundred fifteen pounds of him looked good. She was about to turn around and run the hell up out of there. Instead she took a deep breath, bit her bottom lip and walked over to the table. He stepped from behind the table and hugged her. He smelled so good. He always did. She pulled away from him and sat down. "Where is Eric?" He asked as she sat down. "We are not here to talk about him, if we are then I'll just... HE cut her off. "Look fuck him, In need you to know that I love you, I always have but you just wouldn't give me the time of day Vicki. I could tell you were hurt at the party, I could see that phony ass nigga tryna' front." "Thomas what is your point? You are about to marry Gloria, I can't change that." He folded his hands in the praying position and put them up to his lips. "Gloria is very special to me. I care a lot about her. She is good for me and to me. You made it crystal clear that I wasn't the one you wanted, and well I have some pride. I'm trying to get my life together. Become legit. I want a wife, a family, and a home. You knew all of this." Thomas had told Vicki this before. She just didn't believe he would ever change. She also thought she would always have him. She continued to chase James. A man who would use her and turn on her. Then Eric, a man who would take her heart and give her nothing in return. Now she realizes Thomas is the one for her and she can't have him. "Thomas look, I love you. I wish I told you sooner but I didn't. It's okay, huh, I'm okay. You have Gloria, and I have Eric." She didn't know how true that part was. "We just missed each other, I messed up, and I let the window close. Time has passed. We need to get over the past and work on our futures." They sat there in silence. When the waitress came Vicki declined a drink. "Vicki, you will always have a special place in my heart. I am going to treat Gloria right though' she deserves that." "I know, that's how you are Thomas, I wouldn't expect anything less." She got up and started walking out. She stopped mid way and with out turning around said, "have a nice life Thomas."

CHAPTER 11

New Years Eve, Thomas and Gloria's wedding day. Vicki was all alone. She had spent Christmas at her parents. Vicki was officially moved out and Brenda and Veronica officially moved in. Vicki and Brenda were getting along okay, they tolerated each other. Vicki dressed up in a navy blue suit that looked more like she was going to work than a wedding. She drove to the hotel to attend the wedding reception. "I can do this," She told herself over and over. When she walked into the lobby there was a sign that read Mr. and Mrs. Thomas A. Jones. She didn't see Gloria or Thomas anywhere. This was too much for Vicki, she wasn't ready. She turned to leave and ran right into Gloria. "Vicki hi, oh my God where is Eric?" They hugged. Gloria looked beautiful. "He's still out of town, He'll be back next week. Where is Tho…uh Avery?" He's out front checking the airline reservation. We're going to Jamaica. He is so wonderful." Vicki felt like crying, but she was truly happy for Gloria. Just then some guy dressed in a tuxedo came and pulled Gloria on to the dance floor. Vicki leaned up against the wall and covered her face with her hands. She turned to the door again to leave and was standing right in front of Thomas. "What are you doing here Vicki? Why are you doing this?" He had a look of disappointment on his face. She ran up the hall and out the door. She stopped to catch her breath. She knew the days of Thomas chasing her were over. She could never have him now. She went back to the apartment and cried the New Year in alone. Thomas was on his way to Jamaica with his new wife, and to top it all off Eric hadn't even called.

Every time Vicki went to work she had to see Thomas and Gloria's wedding picture. Thomas had opened a clothing store of his own called *Gear Up.* He even had his own line of clothing called *TAJ APPERAL.* He made good on his word to become legit. As long as Gloria didn't talk about Thomas things were okay. Which was pretty rare. She constantly invited Eric and Vicki to join them for dinner or a night out. Vicki always had an excuse. She may have excepted them being married, but she wasn't about to start spending time with the newlyweds. It had been over a year now and Eric still hadn't made any advancement toward a divorce. He started spending more and more time in New

York. Vicki wasn't up for pretending to be the happy couple when she knew Thomas and Gloria had the real thing.

Friday when Vicki got off work she went shopping for groceries for her mother's house. With Brenda and Veronica staying there and Vernon the only one working, things were kind of tight. Veronica had taken over Vicki's room. What was once a white comforter with green floral print was now a pink comforter with a big purple dinosaur. She even had the curtains to match. It was all too cute. When Vicki pulled up to her mother's house Shan came out and over to Vicki's car. "Vicki hi, long time no see." Shan looked different. Maybe because Vicki hadn't seen her in a while. "Vicki I am back in school. Working on my cosmetology license. I'll be finished in three months." Vicki forced herself to smile. "Good Shan, good luck with that." "Vicki you inspired me. You really have yourself together, you know, and you seem so happy. Your job, your man, I mean life is going really well for you." Shan had no idea how miserable Vicki really was. The only thing she had positive in her life now was her job, but with having to see

Gloria everyday, even that wasn't the best. "Vicki, I know we been through some real shit, but I am trying. I am really sorry. I swear I am. I miss you so much. You are my only friend. I need you." Shan pushed her bangs behind her ear. That was it, that's why she looked different she had let her hair grow back.

Vicki missed Shan too. "Shan, I just have a lot I am dealing with right now. You and James, well that really hurt. I am just not certain I could deal with your relationship." Shan shook her head in agreement. "I understand, but there is no relationship. There never was. I had told him I thought I was pregnant and he took off. Wouldn't take my calls wouldn't return my calls. He's seeing somebody else now. He always was. One night we were getting busy, and that bastard must have called me your name." Vicki wanted to smile. It took every bit of self-control she had not to. "You know you want to smile bitch. It's okay, I am over it." They started laughing. "Shan call me, we'll go out this weekend. I really miss you. They hugged and Shan ran back across the street to her apartment. Vicki felt good. If she rebuilt her friendship with

Shan she would have someone to talk to. When she walked into the house her mother was passed out on the couch. The house was a mess. Toys everywhere. "Brenda, where are you?" Brenda came into the kitchen and started helping her put up the groceries. Veronica came running in behind her. "Auntie Vicki, hi." She jumped up and hugged Vicki. Brenda was leaning against the sink, eating an apple that Vicki had just bought. Vicki put Veronica down. "Ronnie, go put your toothbrush and pajamas in your bag I gave you, I want you to come stay with me tonight. She started clapping her hands and took off out the kitchen. Brenda rolled her eyes. "Take her little bad ass, please." Vicki looked Brenda up and down. She was so tacky. She was wearing and old tee shirt and some dirty sweat pants. "Have you been looking for a job Brenda, or enrolled in school? Vernon can't do it all by himself." "Well, I be taking care of Veronica all day, so he ain't doing it all by himself." She took another bite out of her apple. "Well, what about cleaning up the house, so Vernon doesn't have to come home to a mess after work. Brenda sucked her teeth and put her hands on her hip. "Every time I do pick something up

Ronnie come right behind me with some more mess, and Vernon is a grown man, he ain't no better than her. Then yo' mama come home drunk as hell and pass out all over the house…" She kept talking but Vicki couldn't hear her. She just saw her lips moving, and her head twirling around on her neck. Who did this trifling heifer think she was living up in my mothers house, eating an apple I just bought, and talking about my mother like she was a drunk off the streets. She tried to take another bite of the apple and Vicki slapped her so hard it flew across the kitchen. "Auntie Vicki." She turned around to see her niece standing there with a bag on the floor and her shoes on the wrong feet. She walked over to her and picked her up. "Put my baby down, you ain't taking her no where." Brenda was screaming like she had lost her mind. She started trying to pull Veronica out of Vicki's arms. Vicki wouldn't let her go. She was about to put her down and been the shit out of Brenda, and the door opened. It was Vernon. "What the hell y'all doing? Give me my daughter." They stopped tugging on her and Vernon snatched her out of Vicki's arms. Vicki and Brenda were standing there in the middle of the kitchen huffing and puffing like they just had a schoolyard brawl. "You ain't taking my baby no where Vicki, you think you better than everybody cuz you graduated and some dope dealer gave you a car. You can't come up in here slapping on me. I live here." "This my mother house Brenda, and I'll put cha' dumb ass out." "Shut up, both of y'all, shut the hell up arguing in front of Veronica like that." Veronica put her head on Vernon' shoulders like the whole scene was effecting her. "Ronnie you want to go with your Auntie Vicki?" She looked up at Brenda then at Vicki and shook her head yes. Vicki reaches for her and they walked out the door. Before she closed it she looked back and said, "You need to tame your bitch Vernon." She slammed the door. She heard Brenda yelling, and her mother never moved. Vicki strapped Veronica into the seat belt and decided to take her shopping. What better place than *Gear Up*.

Thomas had three stores in California now. One in San Francisco, one in Oakland, and one in Los Angeles. Gloria told Vicki he was opening his next store in Atlanta, Georgia. Vicki was very proud of Thomas. She hadn't seen him since his wedding night around four months ago. Vicki went to the store in the downtown San Francisco area. She knew that Thomas would be there. That was the main store. After switching Veronica's shoes to the right feet they got out of the car. It was very busy. Everyone who worked in the store was black. Vicki wasn't surprised. When they walked in a young brother greeted them. He was dressed in *TAJ APPERAL*. Vicki had to admit, Thomas had come a long way, and he did a good job. His line of clothing had been featured in al of the urban and hip-hop magazines. The store was set of in sections. Men's, women's kids, and coats. The kids' section was in the back of the store by the fitting rooms. As Vicki walked to the back of the store looking for the manager's office she started feeling guilty. She spotted a pair of overalls. They were blue jeans with Thomas's logo on them. She pulled them off the rack and held them up to Veronica. When she looked up, Thomas was looking down at her. She stood up. "Uh, Thomas, hi, I didn't think you'd be here." She lied. "Vicki, what are you doing here?" "I was shopping, what do you think. I thought I would give you some business." "I don't need your business Victoria." She took a deep breath, cleared her throat, and put the overalls back on the rack. "Fine, I'll leave." She stormed to the front of the store and realized she walked off with out Veronica. She tuned back and Thomas was holding her. They just stared at each other. "Come in my office Vicki." He sat behind his desk, which was cluttered with paper. "Thomas look…" Vicki tried to speak but he interrupted her. "Vicki, I just don't understand you. Before I was with Gloria, I had to almost beg you to spend any time with me. Now you like, well you know, all at me and you know I am not available. What's up with that?" Veronica was sitting in the chair next to her. "Thomas before, I just didn't know what I wanted. I was busy chasing dreams. I just took you for granted and thought you would always be there. I just can't stop thinking about you. I have tried." Thomas covered his face with his hands. Vicki saw his wedding ring. She swallowed hard. "Thomas I don't want to hurt Gloria, she is really great, and a good friend. I can't shake these feelings." "What about this man Eric, Gloria tells me you are so in love with him, waiting for a proposal." "Well he's there yeah, but it's not you, when he holds me I think about you. He's not mine though, never really was. He's married with a child. They live in New York." Thomas shook his head. "Vicki, you had…look, I am not leaving Gloria, and I will not hurt her. She has helped me grow so much." "I know that, but I wanted you to know how I felt, I shouldn't be here." The door flew open, it was Gloria. "Why shouldn't you be here, why are you here?" Thomas stood up so abrupt that his chair flipped over. Gloria looked from Thomas to Vicki then to Veronica. "Hey babe." Thomas came from around the desk after standing his chair up. "Vicki came to shop and see the store with her niece." "Yeah, and I uh was asking Avery if he could hook my brothers girlfriend up with a job. We just had this big argument at my moms house because she stays there and won't help out." Vicki took a deep breath. That was a good one she told herself. "Oh Vicki," Gloria kissed her on the cheek. She reaches for Veronica. "I'm Ronnie" Thomas and Vickie laughed nervously. Hoping that was all Veronica had to say. "Well hello Ronnie, I'm Gloria, why don't we go and get some ice cream and let your aunt Vicki, and Avery talk. Veronica started clapping and yelling "ice cream, ice cream". Gloria pinched Veronica's nose. "Okay, babe, she kissed Thomas. You two finish talking, we'll back shortly. Gloria walked out with Veronica in tow. Dang Vicki thought, why did Gloria have to be so sweet. Thomas and Vicki just stared at each other. Vicki spoke first. "Thomas look this is crazy, telling lies to Gloria and sneaking around town trying to run in to you. This is just not me." "That is what I have been trying to figure out Vicki, look it's a situation you put yourself in, and you have to deal with it." He looked at her really closely. "Does Vernon's girl really need a job?" Vicki thought about it for a moment. Yes Brenda needed a job, but why should she help her. Thomas must of read her mind. "Vicki, I know you never liked that girl, but I know what is going on with your dad bailing out and all. Vernon can't carry that load, and he's making some bad decisions just trying to stay above water. Tell her to come down to the store Monday, and we'll work something out." "Okay Thomas, Thank you" Vicki stood up and then Thomas stood up. "Thomas I will not bother you any more this is it. I'm going to just have to deal with seeing your wedding picture everyday, and get over it." Thomas shook his head. "That's about to change. You see, Gloria will be giving you two weeks on Monday. She has a business degree and we are going to put it to use. She's going to help me run the stores."

"Fine, that will make it all the more easy. I'll send Brenda down Monday, oh, and I'll take the overalls I picked up." Thomas handed her a *Gear Up* bag. "I threw in the shirt to match." He gave her half a smile as if he was almost embarrassed. Vicki took the bag and smiled back. She left his office and went to pick up Veronica from the ice cream parlor where she was eating ice cream with Gloria. She felt better.

CHAPTER 12

Two weeks had passed; it was Gloria's last day at work and Brenda's firs day. She was going to be working in the San Francisco office as a floor monitor. Vicki had an appointment today with TreVeon, Eric was back, but besides sex, him and Vicki didn't do anything. Not even eat dinner together. Vicki had so much going on at once in her life she developed chronic headaches. Today she was just going to focus on TreVeon.

He was excited about his session today. Vicki had took a chance and called his mother one day. She had been communicating with her for over a month now. Today he and his mother were going to have their first conversation in over two years. When Mr. spoons brought him into the office he didn't speak to Vicki. He took the handcuffs off and turned and walked out. Vicki and TreVeon laughed. "How are you today Tre?" "Nervous as hell, I ain't talked to my moms in a while. I can't believe she wants to talk to me." "Well she is equally as nervous as you, she is also wondering how you are. She says she really misses you. But I'll let her tell you all of this. "Well if she had kept in touch and worried about me like a natural mother I wouldn't be here. But men always came first with her." "Remember we talked about harboring those feelings. You need to talk about this some more before we call?" "Na, I'm cool with it, you know I heard she got a new cat living up with her. I just don't want the same trouble. Some cat whipping on my moms." "Well they are married and she appears to be happy." He sat in silence for a moment. "Well if she is, she is, I just ant to be close to my mother like we use to be." Vicki understood that. She missed her mother to. "Well let's make the call. TreVeon wasn't allowed to have the number so Vicki dialed. A man answered. "Yes, my name is Victoria Dupree, May I speak with Evelyn Spencer?" She smiled at James. He was looking at her with those light brown eyes and long lashes. After a few seconds a woman got on the line. "Good morning Victoria, This is Evelyn." "Hello Evelyn." TreVeons eyes lit up. "I have TreVeon here, he is very excited to speak with you." Vicki handed him the phone. "Hi Ma, I am doing okay and you…and you are married now…Melvin, I see…" Vicki listened to TreVeon talk to his mother. It made her want to run out of the office and call her own mother. She noticed that he smiled the whole conversation. "I know you do, I love you too." They hung up and from the look on his face the conversation went well.

There was a going away party for Gloria in the employee lounge. Not much of a party. People came by got cake to go, and barely wished her well. Vicki promised to keep in touch with Gloria. She knew that she would not. This was for the best she told herself. Loose a friend to save her own guilty self. The selection process for Vicki was not easy. She went through a temp agency and nobody she interviewed seemed to work out. She finally settled on a young black man, Theodore Clark. He and Vicki hit it off well. The interview was ore like two old friends who hadn't seen each other while. Ten minutes into the interview when he knew he had Vicki, he let it go. "Call me Teddy Ms. Thing, and I hope you don't mind I will not be in a suit and tie every day. This was for the interview, but believe me I can dress." Vicki had to admit he was styling in his navy blue Armani suit and tie. The boy had it going on. He was very handsome, and if you didn't know him you would think he was a good catch for a woman, but when he let it go, he let it go.

Vicki and Teddy had hit if off big time. He was very efficient, and very neat. He was also fun to chill with. Vicki and Shan had gone out with him a couple of times and once went on a shopping spree at the expense of one of Teddy's boyfriend's credit card. He kept Vicki in stitches. One night when she was out with Shan and Teddy, Gloria called and invited her and Eric to join her and Thomas for dinner. Eric had excepted the invitation so Friday they were going to be going out. Vicki had started thinking about Thomas less and less and she was working hard at getting along with Eric. They were going to meet with Thomas and Gloria at a place called Bon'Appettite. Vicki wanted to fake sick but what the hell, this was a way to see if she was finally over Thomas. They managed to make it to the place before Thomas and Gloria. Vicki told Eric she only wanted dinner, and she wanted to leave afterward because she wanted him for desert. He smiled and agreed. He leaned over and gave her a kiss. Thomas and Gloria walked in. "Are we interrupting something?" They stopped kissing. Vicki and Eric stood up. The men shook hands, and Eric kissed Gloria on the cheek. "You look great Gloria, it's good to see you two again." Eric was being his usual charming self for company. She did look absolutely stunning Vicki thought. Her and Gloria hugged and they all sat down. Thomas hadn't said too much. Dinner went well. Vicki felt okay with this but she was still ready to go. After dinner and two margaritas Eric suggested that they go dancing. Vicki was shocked. She had already told Eric she wanted to go straight home. She shot him the evil eye. Gloria seemed so thrilled with the idea. Thomas just shrugged his shoulders and they were off. They went to a small club out in Oakland; it was more of a social mix than any thing. The dance floor was very small. They got a booth over looking the dance floor. The waitress came over and took drink orders. Eric ordered another margarita. Thomas ordered a virgin daiquiri for him and Gloria. Vicki ordered herself a rum and coke. They started playing this is how we do it. Eric asked Vicki to dance. "Not this one honey, I want to get my drink first." "I'll dance with you." Gloria took Eric by the hand and they went to the dance floor. Vicki watched the two of them dance. Eric always did move smooth. Gloria couldn't keep up. She danced like a white girl. Eric looked up at Vicki and winked. She smiled and turned to Thomas who was staring right at her. "Why are you avoiding Gloria, she thinks of you as a really good friend you know." Vicki frowned at Thomas. "I think of her as a really good friend to. That's why this hasn't been easy for me. But as you can see, I am trying to deal with it." "You still seeing that sucka?" Before she could respond the waitress came with the drinks, and Gloria and Eric were right behind her. *You are my lady* by Freddie Jackson came on and Eric grabbed Vicki's hand and they went to dance. Before she left she shot Thomas and evil eye. Eric held Vicki close. He kissed her ear and her neck. He looked her in the eyes. "Vicki I know you want what Avery and Gloria have. I sear we will get there soon. Vicki felt her legs get weak and Eric squeezed her tighter. "Don't be afraid to be with Gloria because of our situation. She wanted me to tell you she loves you and you can talk to her about anything." "She said that Eric?" "Yes Vicki she misses you and she wants you two to be friends. I know you have been avoiding her because, well she wanted me to tell you that." He kissed her long and passionately and she started falling in love with him all over again.

CHAPTER 13

Monday morning when Vicki arrived at work Teddy had the radio blasting more bounce to the ounce. "Hey Miss Thing, make it bounce." Vicki started laughing and walked past Teddy into her office. "Turn in down Theodore, you not at home." He turned it down and followed her into her office. You have two messages. One is from that fine man of yours." She snatched the messages out of his hand. "Back off Teddy, he is not available." He smiled at her and walked back out of her office. The message from Eric was asking her to meet him for lunch. She could hardly contain her smile. The smile quickly faded. Eric asking to meet her for lunch wasn't always good news. He was probably going out of town again. The other message was from Evelyn, TreVeons mother. She called her immediately. Evelyn wanted Vicki to schedule a hearing so that she could talk about having TreVeon released back into her custody. They had been communicating now through letters and phone calls and she was ready to build a relationship with her son.

Eric met Vicki at a Chinese restaurant called Tai Wans. After they talked about how each person was doing at work

Eric looked Vicki in her eyes. She put her chopsticks down. "So, what's the news Matthews?" He pulled black velvet box out of this inside jacket pocket. He opened it up. It was an engagement ring. Vicki bit her bottom lip and tears welled up in her eyes. He actually got down on one knee. "Victoria will you marry me?" She was shaking her head yes before he finished the question. "Yes, I will." He got up and pulled her into his arms. She didn't even think about his wife or daughter in New York.

After work she was going to Shan's shop to get her hair done. Shan had finished school and was working in one of the most popular shops in San Francisco. Vicki sat there and listened to all the latest gossip. She was Shan's last customer. After she washed and flat ironed Vicki's hair they left together. "Girl, Eric still wont ride in this car?" Shan asked as they cruised up the freeway headed towards Shan's apartment. "Girl, Eric will not even put his head in the window of this car let alone ride in it." Vicki cleared her throat. "Shan, girl I'm getting married." Shan shot her head around. "To who Eric?" Vicki screamed and flashed her ring to Shan. "Yes of course Eric, who else?" She waived her left hand in front of Shan's face wiggling her fingers. Shan took the ring off of Vicki fingers and examined it. "What about his fucking wife Vicki? Have you forgotten the bastard is still married?" Shan wasn't trying to hurt Vicki she was just tired of Eric stringing her along. This is probably just another ploy to hold onto Vicki while he continued doing what ever he wanted to do Shan thought to herself. "Shan why you want to ruin my news and bring that up. Damn." She took her ring back and put it back on. "Vicki you know I am happy for you but you can't ignore the fact that he is still married with a child. Marriage is real girl, make him be real." Vicki pulled up in her mother's driveway. Her and Shan got out of the car. "Vicki, look I am happy for you. I can't wait to get started with the planning." They hugged and Shan ran across the street. Vicki yelled out to her. "Call me Shan" Shan turned around. "Yeah, I'll call you…a bitch." They laughed and went inside.

As usual the house was a disaster. No one was home. Vicki picked up Veronica's toys and vacuumed the living room. She swept the kitchen floor and washed the dishes.

She cleaned her mother's room and cleaned the bathroom. After she finished she lay across her mother's bed and closed her eyes. Before she knew it she was sleep. She woke up to the phone ringing. She eyed the alarm clock on her mother's nightstand. It read 10:37. "Hello" She picked up the phone in her mother's room. It was Eric. "Vicki this is Eric. Why didn't you call me and tell me you weren't coming home?" Vicki rubbed her eyes. "Sorry honey I came over and cleaned up the house. I had to lie down for a minute and I guess the time got by me. I'm on my way now." What am I going to do with you girl? Hurry up and drive safely." He kissed into the phone and hung up. After she hung up with Eric the phone rang again. "Yes" "Vicki, this is Vernon, what are doing there?" "Dang Vern, I can't come see my family no more, where is everybody?" "Veronica is with Brenda mother, and it aint no telling where ya mama is. Brenda should be there by now. She got off at nine thirty. Oh yeah, thanks for hooking her up with the job. I can see you still got pull with Thomas." Vicki let out a deep sigh. "Anyway, I miss you Vern, let's do something this weekend." "Yeah, we'll see what's up, get at me." After she hung up with Vernon she realized she missed him. She forgot to tell him her news about being engaged. Oh well she thought, she'll tell him later, for now she was going home to her fiancée' She kissed her ring and headed home.

Vicki went to the hearing with TreVeon, Evelyn, and Tony Spoons. Vicki filed petitions on TreVeon's behalf. Stating how he has made tremendous progress. How he longs to be home with his mother and how they have been communicating, and his mother is the one who requested he be detained now wants him home. Vicki waited outside the room where the hearing was to take place. A woman approached her. "Hello, I am here for a hearing for my son. Can you…" "You must be Evelyn. Hello I am Victoria and very pleased to meet you." Vicki held out her hand. She blinked her eyes several times. You're Victoria Dupree?" Vicki knew then where TreVeon got his eyelashes. Evelyn was beautiful. She had a small round nose and her eyes were slanted upward. She looked like a black china doll. Her skin was like smooth black silk. You could see in her eyes she has been though a lot. Although very attractive, she had a worried look about her. "The hearing is right in this room." They walked in together and sat side by side. TreVeon came in with Tony Spoons and he was in handcuffs. Vicki could see that bothered Evelyn. HE noticed the two sitting together and winked his eye. They both smiled. "Gosh Victoria that boy has grown into quite a handsome young man, he looks just like his father winking those deadly eyes." She had tears in her eyes. Vicki placed her hand over Evelyn. "He is a very special young man Evelyn, very bright. He has a lot of potential. He just needs a chance." The judge came in and they began to discuss the boy's life like he wasn't even in the room. The petitions were viewed previously by the judge, so he just needed to hear what each person had to say. A man assigned to help TreVeon spoke first. "He has less than a year your honor, and his mother wants him home. His counselor says he has made great progress with his temper and he is showing remorse for what happened. She is willing to continue to meet with him after his release. I see no reason why petition for early release isn't granted. After all he's serving time at the request of his mother, who was the one that initially requested he be detained by the state." The woman assigned to speak against him spoke next. "Well you honor he hasn't been meeting with this new counselor for that long and according to the files before hers TreVeon is very violent, consider his history. He has tried to escape from here more than once and his probation officer says he is more than rebellious against authority. I think it will be in his best interest to serve out the remainder until his eighteenth birthday. Apparently meeting with the counselor is doing him some good, so he needs to continue to see her. Meeting with her after release is not an option. The counselor is for the children in the center." They went back and forth over releasing him to his own mother. Vicki looked over at Mr. Spoons and he blew her a kiss. The judge asked Evelyn if she had anything to say. "Yes, I know I have made mistakes as a parent. I missed a lot of my son's life, and I want him home now. I want to make up for lost times and catch up on his life." She stayed standing. The judge smiled at her. "You can sit down now. Well the files from his previous counselor to his current one are so different it makes me leery about just releasing him. TreVeon can have weekend passes to visit with his mother. After he graduates, if he does so with a 3.0 or better he will be free to go. If he even looks like he is about to get out of line, or even jay walk, the passes are canceled. Is that clear Mr. Spencer?" "Yes sir, crystal clear, thank you." Vicki gave Evelyns hand a tight squeeze. She felt good.

CHAPTER 14

Vicki was at home preparing to go to TreVeons graduation. He made it and was graduating with a 3.83. Afterward there was to be a celebration at his mother's house. Since he had started getting his weekend passes; his relationship with his mother was great. He was even getting along with her new husband. Vicki had asked Eric to go but he refused. Said he was working late.

After Vicki showered, she did her makeup and dressed in her underwear and pantyhose. She checked her hair that Shan did for her last night. It was still intact. She was putting on her shoes when there was a knock at the door. She grabbed Eric's black silk robe and tied it at the waste. She opened the door. "Since when did Eric have a maid, and when did she start wearing the robe I gave him for Christmas?" Vicki swallowed hard and clutched the robe at the top and pulled it closed tighter. "Excuse me." Vicki said. Thoughts raced in her mind. Voices, faces, places, she ran all through her memory bank and came up with nothing. "This is Eric Matthews apartment, is it not?" Vicki still searching her memory bank answered "it is, and mines how can I help you?" The woman smiled and then it hit Vicki like a ton of bricks. It was Naomi, Eric's wife. "You can get the hell out of my husbands apartment bitch." Then she pushed her way in and started looking for the phone like she owned the place. Vicki went into the bedroom and threw on some sweats and a T-shirt and took the pumps off just in case. When she came back into the living room the woman was yelling into the phone "Right now damn it." then she slammed the phone down and looked over at Vicki. "Well Ms. Lady we are two adults so let's act like it." She looked Vicki up and down. I am Naomi Matthews; I am Eric's wife. You can either get what ever belongs to you now and leave or you can wait for Eric to come and throw you out." Who the hell did she think she was talking to like her child? "Well Naomi, you can't be much of a wife if Eric is asking me to marry him." Vicki flashed her engagement ring in her face. She smiled and shook her head. "Is that what Eric gave you, you have a lot to learn." She took deep breath. "You call that an engagement ring. That is a piece of shit. I knew he was out here screwing some one, but damn he really has you fooled. I am sorry if he made you any promises sweet heart, look honey this is a ring." She flashed her hand in Vicki's face and the rock on that ring nearly blinded Vicki. Not to mention the stones surrounding it. It made Vicki's ring look like it came from the bubble gum machine. Vicki tried to slap her hand out of her face but she moved it too soon. She rolled her eyes and shook her head in disgust at Vicki. She picked up her bag that she had dropped by the phone and went into the bedroom and slammed the door. Vicki stood there with her mouth open in shock not knowing what to do. She thought to herself, this is my house. She went to the bedroom door to put her out but the door was locked. "Get the hell out this is my house bitch." She felt like a kid pounding on the door yelling at this woman. She went and sat down to wait for Eric. "Hmmm, now is a good as time as any to tell her he wants a divorce."

Eric opened the door looking like he just ran a marathon. He was breathing hard and his tie had been loosened. Vicki stood up. The bedroom door opened. Naomi walked into the living room and stood next to Vicki. Eric stood there with a confused look on his face. Vicki spoke first. "Well Eric, here is your chance to tell her it is over." Naomi crossed her arms at her chest. Eric ran his hand over his hair. "Vicki I thought you were going to the graduation party for that kid Trevor, what are you doing here?" His name is TreVeon and I live here damn it skip all that and get to the matter at hand." He continued to look dazed, and he just stared at Vicki. "Eric, hello, I came in on an earlier flight and wanted to surprise you. Surprise!" She squealed and smiled. He mumbled under his breath. "Yeah, you ain't never lied." "I just got off the phone with daddy, he wants us to come over tonight and sign the lease papers on the apartment, and renew your benefits package. Oh and he was just so happy to see Erica. She's over there now, him and mother figured we would want some time to ourselves so they kept her. Now that I have taken care of that child you take care of this one." She pointed at Vicki. Eric looked at Vicki but he didn't speak. She was crushed. How could he not defend her? " You poor pathetic excuse for a man. I am not the child here, you are. I'll make this easy on you Eric. I'll just leave." Vicki walked around Naomi and into the bedroom. She put on her sneakers and grabbed her purse. She walked back out into the living room. "Ill be back tomorrow to get the rest of my things. You Ms. Naomi, you are some piece of work. Treating this man like a puppet because your daddy gives you the strings to pull. But I guess if he allows it. Two pathetic ass holes deserve one another." She walked out and slammed the door she. She passed Eric's Lexus and pulled the umbrella out of her trunk and busted the windows. It felt good but she still felt awful.

She drove to her mother's house in tears. When she reach her mothers house, her mother was on her way out of the door. Vicki jumped out of the car and ran into her mother's arms. "Oh mom" Victoria are you all right, honey what is it?" "It's Eric mom, me and Eric it's over." She started crying out loud. They held each other on the porch until Vicki got her crying under control. She stopped crying aloud but the tears kept coming. They went into the house and into Vicki's mother's bedroom. She made tea for her and Vicki and they talked and bonded and cried together just like old times.

The next day Vicki took Vernon with her to the apartment to get her things. Everything was already in boxes. She started to cry all over again. "Stop it Vicki, let all that crying shit go. Let's just get your shit and get out. It's over." "I know Vernon but all this time, I gave him everything and I am suppose to just walk away. No Vernon this is my house, and my man." She sat on the couch. Vernon snatched her up by the arm. "He aint yo' man Vicki, he never was the nigga is married. You knew that, you set yourself up, you should have been expecting this." He grabbed up two boxes and a bag and walked out the door. He couldn't stand to see his sister like this and when he seen Eric his ass was going to be out. She wanted to destroy the apartment. But what good would it do. Vernon was right. She knew this all along but it didn't make it hurt any less. She looked at the ring on her finger. She took it off and put it on her right hand. No need in giving it back. He wasn't going to give back shit she gave him. Vicki picked up a box and followed Vernon out. She was going to be staying with Shan until she found her own place. She wanted to stay with her mother, but she couldn't bare the thought of staying in the same house as Brenda. Across the street would be just fine. But would she?

CHAPTER 15

Vicki took three weeks off of work. She mostly just hung out with Shan in the shop, helping with shampoos, sweeping up hair and picking up on the latest gossip. Eric had been by her mothers' house several times. He was fortunate enough to miss Vernon each time. Her car was parked in her mother's garage so he had no idea she was right across the street. Though' he did call Shan house once. She told him off so bad, Vicki knew he wouldn't call back there. There were more motherfuckers, and bitch ass niggas than Vicki ever heard. It was almost funny. Vicki even went to dinner one evening with TreVeon and his mother Evelyn. They were doing just fine. She convinced her mother to go to re-hab and she was going to AA meeting s faithfully. Everyone was doing fine except Vicki.

The weekend before she was to go back to work her and her family were going out to dinner for Veronica's fourth birthday. Of course Brenda didn't plan her a party. "McDonalds, I want McDonalds, Veronica was yelling. Vicki was more in the mood for lobster, but since it was Veronica's birthday chicken nuggets it was. Vicki was holding Veronica in her lap, and Shan's son was playing Vernon's play station. Brenda and Vernon were sitting on the couch watching. Shan was working late and would try and meet them there. They were all sitting around waiting on Beverly, Vicki and Vernon mother. She had been gone in Vernon truck all day. At 8:30 the phone rang. Veronica answered. "Hello, Hi nana, it's my birthday you not coming? Vicki, Yeah hold on. Auntie it's nana.She handed the phone to Vicki. "Ma where are you, we have been waiting on you for over an hour now…fine it's your grandbaby's birthday but what ever." She hung up the phone. "Let's go, she's not coming." They piled in Vicki's car and Veronica sat in the front seat. Vernon pulled Vicki's hair. "Where yo' mama?" Vicki looked back and rolled her eyes. "Take a guess." Vernon sat back and let out a sigh. Vicki couldn't stop thinking about her mother. She could tell from the noise that she was in a bar. She couldn't even sing happy birthday and she only ate one of her chicken nuggets. She wanted to just go home and get in her bed, and lay in her mans arms. Then she remembered, she had no home, no bed, and no man to go to. She had a sofa in her best friend's apartment.

When they pulled up to her mother's house she had to park on the street. There was a police squad car in her mother's driveway. Vicki threw the car in park and looked back at Vernon. "What did you do?" He cursed under his breath and got out of the car. The officers were on there way back from the door. "Officers can I help you?" They looked Vernon up and down. "Yeah son you can." Vernon sucked his teeth. "Look my name is Vernon, and I aint yo son." By now Vicki was out of the car headed towards the officers. Brenda was getting Veronica out of the seat belt. Officers, I'm Victoria Dupree this is my mothers house is something wrong?" One of the officers recognized Vicki. "Victoria, you work at Y.G.C. I'm Officer Reed." Vicki smiled, she recognized him but she didn't feel like being pleasant with him. "Yes hello, listen is something wrong officer?" He took his hat off and elbowed his partner. He took his off. "Well there's been an accident." Vernon started yelling. "What the fuck is going on?" Vicki started breathing heavy; her chest was starting to feel tight. Brenda just stood there holding Veronica's hand with a blank look on her face. Thoughts started racing in Vicki's head. Marcus Shans son spoke. "Who was in an accident?" The officer looked down at his note pad. "Beverly Dupree" He answered with no hint of emotion. Vernon had tears in his eyes. "That's my mother, is she okay?" Officer Reed shook his head. "She was in a car accident, she didn't make it, we need some one to go down to the city morgue and identify the body, and claim the belongings." Vicki started screaming. She was shaking her head no and yelling. "This is mistake, she can't be no, no please." Vernon tried to hold her and she pushed him away. "No way Vernon hell no this is not happening." "Are you Vernon Dupree Jr.?" The officer was asking. Vernon tried to remain calm and strong but he was crying when he spoke. "Yeah man what you need?" The officer looked down at a note pad and spoke. "The black ford bronco was registered in your name, I'm sorry but it was messed up pretty bad. It's totaled, when you get the time you van pick up the paper work at the station. I'm sorry." They put their hats back on got in their car and drove away. Vicki was standing on the sidewalk in shock.

Brenda was sitting on the front porch holding Veronica and they were both crying. Vernon looked over at Shan son Marcus. "Brenda go in. Take Marcus and Veronica in. We'll be back". He walked over to Vicki and walked with her to the car and sat her in the passenger seat. He got in the driver seat and they were on their way to the city morgue to identify their mother's body. Vicki sat in the passenger seat and cried. "I can't believe it Vernon, please no, please no this can't be happening." Vernon cried silently, as he tried to appear strong for Vicki's sake. But this felt like the hardest thing he'd ever had to do.

Back at home Vernon got out of the car. "Come on in Vicki, get out of the car." Vicki shook her head. "I'll be in later Vernon, I need to think, go on I'll be fine. Go and check on Brenda and the kids." He closed the door and went in the house. Vicki got in the driver's seat and took off. She ended up at Twin Peaks. It was a spot across the street from her old high school and her job that allowed you to view the whole San Francisco, the Bay Bridge, and the entire stretch of the bay. It was a wonderful view. Vicki used to come here with Thomas. One of the other things she took for granted about Thomas was he was a good listener. She came here with Eric once and all he wanted to do was crawl all over her. She sat in her car crying going over events in her life. She wanted to drive off the edge. She got out of the car and walked over to the edge. She looked over all of San Francisco. But she couldn't enjoy any of the view. She felt that some one was watching her. She sat on the edge of the rail. Some one flashed their headlights. She didn't bother turning around. She heard footsteps coming towards her. "Victoria is that you?" It was Thomas. Vicki looked back over her shoulder. "Thomas, hi, yeah it's me." She cleared her throat and wiped her eyes. She stood up. She started crying again. He pulled her to him and held her tight. He walked her over to her car and they got in. "Vicki what's going on?" Vicki told Thomas what happened with her mother, then about Eric. "Damn Vicki, I am so sorry, you shouldn't be alone, come to me and Gloria's house." Vicki's mouth dropped open. It took all her will power not to slap the black off Thomas. "Wait a minute Vicki. Gloria considers you her friend, and she could be a good person to talk to at a time like this. I just don't think you should be alone." Vicki closed her eyes and shook her head. "Thank you Thomas, but no. I can't, I wouldn't feel comfortable. Not under any circumstances. I already feel like I have betrayed her. Besides, I have Vernon and Shan; I'm not alone. I'll be fine." Thomas smiled at Vicki. "Life aint fair baby girl, but you have to play *the hand that's dealt.* So don't throw in your hand just yet, just concentrate on your next play." He looked at her real hard. "Are you sure you are going to be okay?" "Yes Thomas, I'll be fine. Now out I have to get home." He kissed her on the cheek and got out of the car. "Nice car" he said and winked and closed the door. She pulled off and cried some more.

The day of the funeral was the saddest day of Vicki's life. All she could think about was how she hung up on her mother the day of her accident. She wished she could rewind the clock and do it all over again. She would have went to get her mother, she would have never treated her so badly. Her mother had a problem, and Vicki didn't do anything to help her. She only hurt her. She was mad at her mother and her mother was racing home to make it to go out with them. Now she was gone.

At the funeral Vicki didn't move. She set there listening to people talk about her mother and her mother's life. After the funeral, back at her mother's house, people came over to offer condolences and be with her and Vernon. They came with food, food and more food. Vernon was really being strong. He greeted the visitors, made all of the arrangements for the service, he even spoke at the funeral. Vicki couldn't do any thing. After the funeral she sat in a rocking chair in the corner of the living room with her feet folded under her. Shan sat next to her holding her hand. Vicki noticed Vernon hugging a man at the door. It was Thomas. He walked over to Vicki and lifted her out of the chair and hugged her. She knew she was standing and she knew Thomas was holing her but she couldn't feel anything. He sat her back down and she folded her legs back under her. Shan offered Thomas her chair and he sat down in the seat next to Vicki. He was holding her hand. Every so often she would squeeze it to make sure some one was still there. People were slowly leaving and Vicki was glad to see them go. She was exhausted. She was tired of hearing people say they were sorry, and that she would be all right. Every one was gone except for Thomas and Vicki was still in the same spot. Shan and Vernon were in the kitchen cleaning up. Brenda had left to go and pick up Veronica from the baby sitter. Vernon had flat out refused to let her attend the funeral. "My daughter don't need her last memories of her nana in a closed box with a picture." No one disputed his decision. He was after all the only one making them. Thomas turned Vicki's head so that she was facing him. She looked tired. "Vicki, I need to talk to you." She tried to respond, but nothing would come out. Before he could say a word the front door opened. It was Vernon Sr. Vicki jumped up from her seat. She stared at him in dis-belief. She couldn't believe her eyes. She started yelling at him. "Get the hell out, get the hell out!" He stood in the doorway. "Victoria look, don't talk to me like that. I am still your father. I came here to talk to your mother. Now where is she?" Vicki tried to charge towards him and Thomas held on to her. Vernon Jr. and Shan were now standing in the living room. Vernon walked over to his father and stood directly in front of him. He stood about two inches shorter than his father did. He squared off with him. "Look, you can't talk to her, and we would appreciate it if you just left." "Look son, I know you and your sister are bitter towards me now, but we are family and we will get past this. I know you have been the man of the house while I was gone and I am not here to challenge you. I want to speak to your mother and this has nothing to do with you. This is my house." I'm going to have to ask you to move boy." Vernon made a move like he was stepping aside. He socked his father in the face and he fell out of the front door. Thomas rushed over to Vernon and held him from behind. Vernon broke away. He took one of his mother's obituaries and shoved it into his father's chest as he struggled to get up. He read the cover while he sat on his knees. He started sobbing aloud. Vernon Jr. didn't feel sorry for him. He was the one after all that drove his mother to drinking. What ever he was feeling he deserved it. "Why didn't anyone tell me?" He was crying and screaming. Vicki walked over to Vernon's side. Vernon put his arm around her and he said, "We couldn't find you." Then he closed the door in his face.

Vicki looked Vernon in his eyes then collapsed in his arms. He was trying to hold her up but he too felt weak. All of this pressure on him and he couldn't take it any more. He started balling out loud and screaming at God for taking his mother. They collapsed to the floor together cried in each other's arm over the loss of their mother and father.

CHAPTER 16

Over the next two months Vicki occupied her mothers room. Her run-ins with Brenda were very few. Brenda was trying hard. She was walking on eggshells. Dealing with Vernon's mood swings, Vicki not talking at all, and Veronica and her question after question. It was hard for her. She started staying away from the house more and more. Vicki decided it was time for her to move out and let Vernon and Brenda have their own space. She moved into a one-bedroom apartment around three miles from her mothers. It was close but not too close.

One Friday when Vicki walked down to her car after work, there was a note on her car. It was from Eric. *"You are not getting away that easily...I love you"* She ripped the note in half and drove off. She drove to the Cozy Inn and found a booth in the back to unwind. She was sipping her glass of wine when the waitress came over and had a bottle in a bucket of ice. "Ma'am, this is for you." Vicki looked up she thought maybe Eric was following her. "No thank you" Thomas walked over to her table. "It's rude to turn down a gift Victoria." He smiled down at her. The waitress placed the bucket on the table and walked away. Thomas sat down. Vicki hadn't seen him since the fiasco at her mother's house the day of the funeral. It was good to see him. He poured her another drink. "So how are you Thomas, how's Gloria?" Thomas took a deep breath and folded his hands on the table. "I'm fine Vicki, Gloria, well she's pregnant." Vicki raised and eyebrow and then her glass. "Well, well Thomas is going to be a daddy, congratulations." She gulped what was left in her glass in one sip. She hiccuped and stood up. She felt dizzy and swerved a little. Thomas stood up and touched her on the shoulder. "Sit down Vicki, there's more." She rolled her eyes. "Well I am not trying to hear it." "He forced her down gently by pushing her shoulder. "What Thomas, are you trying to see me cry?" He looked away from her for a second then back in her eyes. He scooted in closer to her. "She knows Vicki, Gloria knows everything. She knows we use to be involved. She knows you still have feelings for me, she knows the real reason you were in the store that day with your niece, she knows everything." Vicki tried to slap Thomas but he grabbed her wrist. Thomas looked sad. "She's gone Vicki, she left me." Vicki couldn't believe her ears. She started to feel awful. "Oh Thomas I am so sorry." He let her wrist go. "Yeah me too." "How could you let this happen Thomas? Why did you do that, why did you tell her. She must hate me now, does she?" He shook his head in disbelief. "Damn Vicki everything is not about you." She started to cry. "Look I'm sorry I just lost my wife. She packed up and moved to Tennessee with her sister. All her clothes, stuff, pictures, my unborn child, gone." "This is all my fault, I should have been honest with her in the beginning. We could have avoided this." "It's not your fault Vicki. We were cleaning out an old storage space of mine in the back of the house. She found a box with pictures of you, you and me, cards, letters, just shit I had from over the years from you and me. I had it in a box. She found it. She asked me to be honest. Said if I ever cared about her that I would tell her the truth. So I did." Vicki could tell he was hurt. "When did this happen Thomas?" "It happened the night of your mothers accident. That is why I was up at Twin Peaks. You know that is my thinking spot. Vicki thought she saw a tear in Thomas eye that refused to fall. "Well is Gloria coming back?" "I don't know Vicki. She said she needed time to deal with being a second pick. I tried to convince her that it's her I love but she is having trouble believing me. I can't blame her. She's carrying my child man, I can't believe I fucked this up." She reminded him of what he told her the night of her mother's accident. "Well Thomas what about what ever hand life deals you, you have to play that hand, just don't throw your cards away. Or something like that." Vicki started crying she had had too much to drink. She had almost finished a whole bottle of wine. He half smiled at her trying to use his words and sayings on him. "Come on Vicki, let me take you home. I'll drive you." Thomas opened the car door for Vicki. When Thomas got it he kissed her on the cheek. "Buckle up Victoria." She told Thomas where she lived and they rode the rest of the way in silence. She told Thomas to pull into stall 90. "I'll walk you up and call a taxi. "No go a head Thomas take the car. I'll get it tomorrow." "No, now let me make sure you make it in safely. I am a gentleman." She smiled at Thomas and they got out. When they reach her floor Vicki thought she seen Eric duck around the corner at the end of the hall. She shook her head and guessed the wine was getting to her. She saw a note on her door. She ran to the end of the hall but no one was there. Thomas was reading the note. It read *"Vicki you should be home by now. Oh, I bet you didn't know I knew where you lived. Love E"* Thomas dropped the note and ran to the end of the hall and then out of the building. He didn't see anything. When he cam e back up Vicki had ripped up the note. They went in. Thomas checked the place out. This is a nice little spot you got here Vicki." He sat down on her couch. "I'll be sleeping here tonight." "Thomas please, that is not necessary, I'll be fine." "Vicki, the nigga is obviously crazy, stalking you and shit, so we'll just see what happens tonight." "Thanks Thomas that would make me feel better." Thomas stood up and looked down at Vicki. She started to feel nervous. He pulled her to him and kissed her long and passionately. He picked her up and carried her into her bedroom and laid her on the bed. She sat up and looked at him standing there looking so fine. "Thomas listen, this is not really a good time for either of us. I am not trying to get my feelings hurt." "I'm not trying to hurt you, I'm trying to make you feel good."

"Because Gloria left or you want me." "I've always wanted you."

They spent the entire weekend together. Vicki didn't think about Eric once. Thomas thought a lot about Gloria. The more he thought about Gloria, the more he made love to Vicki. Sunday night Vicki insisted Thomas go home. "I'll be fine Thomas, you can't stay here for ever. Besides Eric isn't going to do anything to me." At the door he looked hard at Vicki. "What do we do now Thomas?" He hugged her. "One day at a time Victoria." He kissed her on the forehead and walked out. When Vicki got to her bedroom there was knocking at the door. She walked back to the door smiling. "I told you go home," she said as she pulled the door open. No one was there. She started laughing. Funny Thomas, hide and seek huh?" Eric came from behind the door. "You found me, or should I say I found you." Vicki tried to close the door but he pushed his way in. "What the hell do you want Eric? Get out, go home." He smiled that perfect smile. "Home is where the heart is baby, I'm at home." He looked tired. His eyes were red and his clothes were wrinkled. "Eric out, go home to your wife." "No, I don't want her, I want to be with you. I need you." He started walking towards her. She put her hands on her hips. "Well I don't want you." He stopped in his tracks. "Why because you have been fucking Thomas. Your best friends husband?" He started coming towards her again. She could smell the alcohol on his breath. "You're drunk Eric, get out." He tried to grab her but she moved back and he fell to the floor. She went into her room to get the phone. He was right behind her. He pushed her on the bed. They wrestled until they fell on the floor and he was on top of her. She tried crawling away from him and reaching the phone. Eric yanked the cord out of the wall. "Who you trying to call, the police, Thomas, your punk ass brother Vernon?" She held the phone above her head and threw it at him. He ducked and it missed him. "Yeah, I'm not that drunk." He grabbed her and threw her down. He held her wrist above her head with one hand and pulled her nightshirt up with the other. She used every muscle in her body to fight him off. He was just too strong. She couldn't believe this. "Eric please you are making a big mistake, you don't want to do this." She was crying and pleading with him. He just looked at her with his evil eyes and grinned while he kneed her in her side trying to get his pants down. She screamed louder. "If you scream one more time I am really going to hurt you, you acting like you never had this before, like you don't want this." She closed her eyes tight and bit her lip. Blood came out she bit so hard on it. Tears were coming down her face. He pulled her underwear to the side and forced his way in. She let out another loud scream. He slapped her across the face. He started pumping harder and faster, Vicki thought he was going to split her in half. Then she felt his release. She felt sick. She just lay there afraid to move. He stood up and pulled up his pants. He looked down at her like he was disgusted with her. "Look what you made me do. I'll leave now but I'll see you later." He walked out rubbing his hand over his head. When she heard the door close she started to cry out loud. She started calling for Thomas. Then she started telling herself that what just happened was what she deserved. She lay in the spot where Eric just raped her and cried herself to sleep.

When she woke up the clock read 3:30am. She got up off the floor and went to take a shower. She ran the water as hot as she could stand it. She balled up the nightshirt and underwear and put them in a plastic bag. She crawled into bed but couldn't fall asleep. At 7:15am her alarm clock went off. She got up and dressed for work. She was in a total state of shock. She took the plastic bag and dropped them in the dumpster. Her knees felt weak. Her eyes were swollen, lip busted and despite an honest effort she couldn't cover up the black eye Eric had given her. She went to work anyway and tried to get by. When she walked in the office, Teddy had the radio blasting as usual. He noticed she wasn't in a good mood and turned the radio down. "Good morning Victoria." She walked past him, into her office and slammed the door."

CHAPTER 17

Two weeks had passed. Around 11:00 Friday morning Teddy started to get really worried about Vicki. She wasn't taking any calls and all of her scheduled appointments had been cancelled. Teddy opened her office door around 4:30. She was just sitting in her chair staring out of the window. He called her name but she didn't respond. He closed the door and called Shan. "Shan this is Teddy, look girl you need to get up here and check on your friend, something aint right." "I thought something might be going on with her. I haven't talked to her in a couple of weeks. I left her several messages. What is she doing now Teddy?" "She just in her office looking out the window. When I went in and called her name she didn't respond. She came in last week with a black eye and a busted lip." Shan yelled at Teddy. "What, and you are just now calling me. I'm on my way." She hung up on him.

Shan came busting through the door. "Where is she now Teddy?" "She still in there, I'm about to head home, so please tell her I hope she feels better or what ever has her like this passes soon" When she opened the door Vicki was just like Teddy had said she'd been all day. Her chair was facing the window with her back to the door. "Vicki, hey, it's me Shan. Where you been girl, you haven't returned any of my calls. Teddy called me said you been acting funny for the last two weeks what's up?" She grabbed the back of the chair and spun it around. Vicki was out cold. Shan shook her and slapped her in the face and she still didn't respond. She checked to hear if she was still breathing and it was like she was barely holding on. Shan looked down and noticed an empty bottle of pills. She picked up the phone and called 911.

She was rushed to emergency where her stomach was pumped. She was going to make it. She came in and out of sleep every so often bus she really didn't know what was going on. She was so embarrassed. She thought to herself, she couldn't get anything right. When she opened her eyes she saw Vernon standing over her bed. Brenda was standing next to him holding Veronica. Shan was on the other side of her bed with tears in her eyes. She wanted to hug everybody. Even Brenda. Thomas was just walking in to the room, she wished the bed would just swallow her up. The doctor walked into the room and Eric was right there with him. Vicki started to breathe heavily. Eric looked at her with a look that could kill. She could almost hear him saying she better not say a word. The doctor smiled warmly at Vicki. "Hello, I'm Dr. Clayton. You gave everyone quite a scare, but you and the baby will be just fine." "Baby!" Eric and Thomas said it at the same time. Everyone in the room had a confused look on their face. "Can we get everyone to leave the room so I can speak to the patient in private." Everyone stepped out of the room. "Victoria, you are somewhere around two weeks pregnant. Your blood work is indicating a low number for the pregnancy hormone, but it doubles daily. You are definitely pregnant." "There must be some mistake doctor, I am not having a baby." "There is no mistake, you are pregnant. Don't worry, it's very early you have plenty options. For now, I would like to recommend Dr. Gene Hardy." There is no need for that, I have my own OBGYN to consult." "No you don't understand, she is a psychiatrist. Now you are a counselor Victoria, you of all people should understand the need to talk to someone when you are having some sort of trouble."

"Trouble, I'm no having any trouble." She said it with irritation in her voice. Who did this man think he was? "Listen, I am not trying to offend you, but I would say attempted suicide by swallowing an entire bottle of pills is a form of trouble or some sort of cry for help." Vicki didn't think of it like that. Was she really trying to kill her self? He scratched a name and number down on a piece of paper and handed it to her. "Look it's up to you, she's an excellent doctor, I highly recommend her." He then walked out of the room. She was about to ball the paper up and the door opened. It was Eric. Vernon was right behind him. "Vicki I will put him out now, just say the word." Eric didn't take his eye off Vicki. "Victoria give me two minutes, okay please just two?" Vicki looked over at Vernon who was standing there with his chest poked out. She motioned him to leave with her head. "I'll be fine Vernon, Two minutes." Vernon blew his breath and walked out the room. "Yeah okay but in two minutes I'll be back up in this piece." Eric walked towards Vicki. She sat up. "Don't take another step, or this whole hospital is going to be trying to pull me off of you." He stopped. "Okay Vicki look, I'm sorry I swear I didn't mean to hurt you. I didn't mean to let that happen. I got carried away. I know you think you hate me now, but you are carrying my child, our child. We can get past this. She looked at him like he lost his mind. "I don't know what kind of sick mind you have Eric, but I wouldn't have your bastard child if it was my last chance. You have two seconds to walk the hell up out of this room and my life or you will regret it." "Vicki, please stop, you can not mean this, you are angry." I came by your office to tell you that Naomi has gone back to New York. That is when Theodore told me the news. Look it is really over between us. I am free now to be with you and just you." "Read my lips you sorry bastard. Get the hell out of my life. I don't want you. I hate you." "Vicki please, I need you." She started yelling at him. "Out, out, you bastard get out." Thomas pushed open the door. He grabbed Eric by the arm and pushed him towards the door. Vernon was standing in the entrance. Eric looked at Vernon. "Excuse me man, your sister wants me out and I'm trying to leave." "Let him out Vernon, just let him go." Vicki spoke just barely above a whisper. Vernon stepped to the side and Eric walked out of the hospital and hopefully out of Vickis life. Vernon walked over to Vicki and kissed her on the nose. You going to be all right?" She shook her head yes, and he walked out of the room.

Thomas sat at the top of the bed and put Vickis head in his lap. He rubbed her back. "We need to talk Victoria. You need to tell me what is going on with you." "Yes Thomas I know, There is a lot you need to know just not now." She cried silently in his lap and thought about what she was going to do. Thank goodness she had Thomas, or did she? She cried harder.

CHAPTER 18

Vicki was suspended from her job for three months. She had to seek out some help with whatever she was going through before she could return. Why did every one keep telling her she needed help? She wasn't crazy, and she didn't need any one trying to convince her otherwise. Teddy cried when she packed up some things. She said she would see him later, but some how he knew they would never work together again. She figured she would just rest for a few weeks and then start looking for a new job. Maybe go back to school for her masters.

Her first week at home she isolated herself from everyone. Thomas stopped by several times. She just wasn't ready to see him. She called Jacobs and Sons and asked for Eric. They said he was transferred to the New York office. She laughed and hung up the phone. Thank God she couldn't believe she was in love with a real live puppet.

Later that night Thomas stopped by again. He had a vase filled with red roses. She contemplated letting him in. He kissed two fingers and placed them on the peephole. He sat the vase down and walked away. Vicki opened the door.

"Thomas wait, please come in." He smiled at her picked up the vase and walked in. "I miss you little girl. Why are you hiding out from the world?" He put the vase on the kitchen counter. He looked Vicki up and down. Her hair was all over her head. She hadn't washed it or combed it since she came home from the hospital. She was wearing a pair of grey sweats and a T-shirt. "You look cute." He started laughing and pulled her in his embrace. He held her tight. They walked to the living room and sat down. "So Thomas I need to know, How's everything with Gloria?" "Well, she is still in Tennessee, the pregnancy is coming along well, and she is going to stay out there and give birth. I think her sister has a lot to do with it. I'll go out there around her due date, to be there for the birth. As far as the marriage goes, well she hasn't said. I think it is pretty much over. She said she feels like I never truly loved her and caring about her wasn't enough." Vicki held Thomas hand. "And me, does she hate me Thomas?" "No, she just wished you were honest with her. She felt as though you two were friends, and well she thinks there was something going on with us more than what I am telling her, because she thinks we were keeping secrets." Vicki covered her face with her hands. "Now you, what was that chump Eric doing at the hospital, did you call him?" "No Thomas, that big mouth Teddy told him when he came by my office." "Well it's a good think that faggot has a big mouth, he saved your life, and our child's." She took a deep breath. "Look Tommy I need to be honest with you. So far dishonesty hasn't paid off. So I am just going to let it all out. Thomas studied Vicki. "Vicki, you aint gone tell me it aint my baby. You slept with Eric again?" "Hold on Thomas let me explain. This is very hard for me." She managed to tell Thomas what happened the night he left. She managed to get it all out with out going into hysteria like she did every time she thought about it. He jumped to his feet and pulled a pistol from the back of his pants. Vicki jumped back into the corner of the couch. Thomas started yelling and waving the gun in the air. "Where he at Vicki, huh, where is he?" "Calm down Thomas and please put that away." He was standing in the middle of her living room with his face in knots and holding the gun. "Don't tell me to calm down. Why didn't you call me, Vernon, the police, somebody? Are you okay?"

Thomas look of anger faded into a look of concern. He put the gun on the table and sat back down next to Vicki. She was trying to deal with this. It felt good to say it out loud. She decided that moment that she would see the psychiatrist that Dr. Clayton recommended. "I'm dealing with it you know. I have to start seeing a head doctor next week, but I don't mind. It'll help me deal with the rape and understand the attempted suicide." "Vicki you don't need no shrink. You all right. You are going to be fine." Vicki shook her head and held Thomas's hand. "It's okay my hob says I need to see one before returning to work and I think it will be a good idea." "Well where is Eric? Don't try and protect him" "He's gone Tommy, I know for sure he is in New York." "Yeah, well I got pull in New York, the big apple aint out of my reach. He could end up missing in a heart beat, or worse." "Thomas please stop, I need your focus to be here. You have enough going on as it is. Besides I don't know whose child I'm carrying." Thomas could barely hear Vicki. She was just speaking above a whisper. He thought he heard her say she didn't know whose child she was carrying. He didn't even think about hat. He hadn't realized he let her hand go. "Listen Thomas, I am not going to have and abortion and I wouldn't go through all of this to give up my baby for adoption. I am keeping it. I won't ask you for any thing. Not even a blood test to help me ascertain who the father is. It's mine and that is all that matters. I'll give the baby my last name." Vicki tried to get up and Thomas held her arm. "Vicki I want to kill him for what he did to you. I know I have my problems to work through with Gloria and all but this, man you…This is just another one of life's hurdles. Fuck a blood test and that baby is going to have his fathers last name, mines. Cuz I know it's my baby okay? Okay?" She shook her head yes. He pulled her close to him and thought about how complex his life had just become. He thought to himself. Damn, the hand that's dealt.

CHAPTER 19

Monday at 11:00am Vicki was to be in the other seat. It was her first session with Dr. Hardy. She already knew about all this stuff and was talking aloud to herself while getting dressed. She's just going to ask me a bunch of questions about my childhood and how I feel about this, that, or the other. How am I supposed to feel? She realized she was talking to herself and grabbed her purse and keys and headed out the door.

When she got to the office it was a little before 11:00. She took several deep breaths and went in. She thought her eyes were playing tricks on her. The woman at the desk looked just like Gloria. She went from the nameplate to the face. It read Loraine Willis, but this was some spooky shit she thought. She stood up and startled Vicki. "I didn't mean to scare you. You must be Victoria Dupree. Dr. Hardy is expecting you. You can go right in." She walked over to the door and opened it. Vicki shook her head and went in. Dr. Hardy was an old white lady with glasses larger than her face. She sat behind a huge oak desk. There were two leather chairs in front of her desk. "Victoria have a seat."

"Please call me Vicki" "All right, and you may call me Gene, or Dr. Hardy which ever you prefer." Victoria sat down. "Okay Dr. Hardy where do we start?" Vicki was starting to feel like this was a mistake. "Where do you want to start?" Here we go Vicki thought. "Well we could start by me telling you I don't think I need to be here. I am only here because my job insisted that before I return I seek out some counseling." "Why don't you think you should be here? You don't think trying to kill yourself is reason enough to seek out some help?" Damn, why do people keep throwing that one mistake in my face she thought? "No, I have friends, family that I could talk to if I need to." "Well perhaps you need someone else to talk to. I mean you did have them before the attempt." Vicki didn't respond. "Do you think this has something to do with the your mother or father?" Vicki went off. "Look lady a man pushed his way into my apartment and raped me is that reason enough?" Vicki put her head down and started crying. "Are you okay? She handed Vicki a tissue. "I'm fine, and I am not reporting it so please don't ask." "That's fine, but would you like to talk about it?" "Hell no, what for so I could get more upset, and what is there to talk about you want details?" "Is he the father of your child?" She was really pushing Vicki thought. She put her head down again; she was determined not to cry again. "Can we change the subject please?" "Yes of course. Why don't you tell me a little about your friends and family you referred to earlier"? For the next forty minutes or so, they talked about Vicki's mother and father. When she left she actually felt better. Like a weight had been lifted from her shoulders. She decided to give the old doctor a chance.

Friday morning Vicki was relaxing in her bed and watching the morning talk shows. Her phone rang. "Hello" "Hey girl, this is Shan, I wish I could lay in the bed all day." "Well I wish I could go to work, what's up?" "Well you know I aint no trouble maker right?" Vicki started laughing. "Anyway tramp, I seen James." "Shan stop right there. We agreed we wouldn't discuss him for one year. That way no feelings will be hurt over what is said or what happened." "Vicki let me finish, I seen him with Brenda. Girl they creeping." Vicki started laughing. Shan was too much. "Shan please, I know you hate both of them and you think Vernon deserves someone better, like you, but this is too much even for you. She is not creeping on Vern, she aint crazy, and if she was that bold it sure wouldn't be with James." "First of all if I wanted Vernon I could have him. Brenda, or no Brenda. I saw her downtown hop in his car and kiss him right in his mouth. Vernon wondering why she always broke, and always late. Hmm, she paying to kick it. Hell he had me kicking him down for a minute." "Shan are you sure, if I bring this to my brother and it's not true he is going to swear I am trying t o break them up." "Vicki, please spare me I don't have to lie" Vicki and Shan went on to talk for the next hour. Shan promised to stop by later if she didn't get off too late.

Around 3:00pm Vicki decided to go shopping. She was coming out of the Disney store and she spotted Brenda coming out of the GAP. She was carrying two huge bags. She almost called Brenda's name but changed her mind. She knew the bags from the GAP weren't for Brenda, because she dressed more like she shopped at Slut's R Us. Vicki decided to pay her brother a visit. When she got to the house Vernon was laid out on the couch watching Jeopardy. "What's up Vern, how you doing on your day off?" He started smiling when he seen Vicki. "What's up bum, how are you doing on your days off?" He got up and hugged her. "So where is Brenda, isn't she off today?" "Yeah, she went to the mall with her friends." "Where she be all the time, she never here." Vernon looked at Vicki strangely. "What's with all the questions on Brenda. Something on your mind?" Vicki paused for a minute. "Well I heard…" The front door opened. It was Brenda. "Hi Vernon, hi Vicki, where is Ronnie?" Now Vernon was really suspicious. Brenda was being polite to Vicki, and where was her bags? "She's at Shan's house, what did you get at the mall?" Vicki butted in. "Yeah, lets see what you bought." Brenda got on the defense. "Damn I didn't see nothing I liked, why, y'all questioning me?" Vernon stood up. "You need to kill that attitude you had lately, a nigga getting tired of all that." Brenda mumbled under her breath. "I'm tired of you." But it wasn't low enough, Vernon heard her. "What you say, you tired of me. Well you can get yo' tired ass out my house. I don't need this shit." Vicki sat on the couch trying to conceal her grin. She stood up. "Okay you two, calm down before you both say something you don't mean." She felt like laughing in Brendas face. "Mind your own business Vicki, you always starting shit between me and Vernon." Before Vicki could respond Vernon said something. "Don't be talking to my sister like that just because you got a fucking attitude." She started to cry. "You and Vicki always be ganging up on me." Vicki could tell from the look in Vernon's eyes he was about to give in. Vernon walked over to Brenda. "Look Bren, I'm sorry. I just been stressing lately." He hugged her and looked at Vicki. Vicki rolled her eyes and stood up. This trifling heifer had her brother whipped. Big bad ass V-Dog as he called himself was whipped. She shook her head and walked out. She was on her way across the street to Shan house. Before she got there Shan was opening her door. "Vernon put that ho out yet, I know y'all seen James just drop her off?" Vicki looked surprised. "Oh she just getting way to bold with it. No I almost told him what you told me, but Brenda came in. Then she got into this heated argument with Vernon and I thought he was about to go off on her, but then she started crying." Shan shook her head. "Mmmm, Vernon can't handle the tears, he done went soft on us." "Well I don't think he is going to put up with her too much longer Shan. I am staying out of it." Shan smiled. "I'm not"

CHAPTER 20

Vicki was almost two months along and Thomas was treating her like she was every bit of nine months. Thomas and Vicki were kicked back in her bed when Thomas pager went off. He checked the number. He just stared at Vicki with a peculiar look on his face. "Is it Gloria Thomas?" He didn't respond, she already knew the answer. She got the cordless phone from the charger and handed it to him. She went into the kitchen to give him some privacy. She poked her head back into the room and smiled at him. "You paying for that call." She winked her eye and closed the door. With out looking back she knew he was smiling. While she was making some tea, she thought back to one of her sessions with Dr. Hardy. They talked about how she would handle the day Gloria would call and ask for Thomas back. Vicki thought she could deal with it. Now she wasn't so sure. She wanted to talk to Dr. Hardy. Today was Tuesday and her appointment wasn't until Friday. She wanted to call her and see if she could see her. No, she thought to her self. Deal with it, What could Gloria want Vicki thought. She hasn't called him in all this time. She's only seven month's so it can't be for the birth. Before the water started boiling in the kettle Thomas came out of the room fully dressed with his keys in is hand. Vicki wasn't sure what was going on and she had a worried look on her face. Thomas spoke. "That was Gloria's sister, there are some complications with the pregnancy. There is a midnight flight leaving tonight, and I'm on it. Reservations have already been made. I have to go." He stood there like he was waiting for Vicki's approval. "So go, have a safe trip. I hope she's okay." Vicki sounded so cold. He walked over to the stove where she was standing and gave her a hug. She didn't return his embrace. He stepped back. "Look Vicki, why are you doing this? You knew that when it was time for delivery I would be going to be with my wife. So don't be trying to make me feel guilty." Vicki felt bad. She was being selfish. "I know, but well I am going to miss you." He hugged her again and rubbed her back. He let her go and walked towards the door. "I love you Thomas, I really do." He stopped at he door and turned around. "Don't worry Victoria you know that I love you right?" She shook her head yes. "I'll call you." then he was out the door. The teakettle whistled and Vicki turned the pot off. She suddenly didn't feel like tea.

Friday Vicki was dressing to go and have her session with Dr. Hardy. She had a lot on her mind. She hadn't heard from Thomas since his plane landed. She tried not to assume the worse. It was after all his wife and his first child. She didn't know if she was carrying his baby or not. She knew her entire hour would be discussing Thomas. She looked forward to letting it all out. When Vicki got to Dr. Hardy's office there was a new receptionist. Vicki just looked at her. She didn't feel like being pleasant. "Victoria Dupree, Dr. Hardy is waiting, you can go right in." Vicki walked in without speaking to her and she heard her suck her teeth. Vicki made a mental note to give her attitude when she left after her session. When she got into Dr. Hardy's office she questioned her about where Lorraine was. "She had a family emergency in Tennessee." Dr. Hardy was talking but Vicki couldn't hear anything she was saying. Tennessee just kept replaying in her head. She blurted out. "Is this some sort of joke. Are you all working together to drive me crazy?" Vicki, what are you talking about? Calm down please." "No don't tell me to fucking calm down. Thomas's wife Gloria lives in Tennessee and Loraine like I told you looks just like her. Now she's gone there." "Vicki a lot of people look alike and well Tennessee is a big place. This is all just a big coincidence. You are being paranoid. Now please calm down and take five deep breaths." She closed her eyes and took five long deep breaths. "Now Vicki, we have made great progress, you know that you can trust me. What is really bothering you?" Vicki stood up and began to pace the floor. "Well, the other day Gloria's sister called Thomas with his plane reservations already made. He took off like a flash. They are claiming complications with the pregnancy." "Why do you say claiming Vicki, you don't believe her, or Thomas?" "Well there hasn't been any trouble so far, and she's seven months. I think it was Gloria who called Thomas." "Why do you think it was her?" "Maybe she wants him back, maybe she made up in her mind that she wants him back." "Wants him back, well he is her husband and you always knew that this was a possibility." Vicki thought to herself how that was true, but she let all this time go by. She couldn't understand. Just like she thought she spent the entire hour talking about Thomas. When the session was over she felt better. She was also hungry. When she walked out she changed her mind about giving the girl attitude. Instead she smiled at her and told her to have a nice day. She saw the surprised look on the girls face and that made her feel even better. She decided to go to the All you can eat buffet for some shrimp and fries.

When she placed her order she was being led to her table by the waiter, and noticed Brenda and James in a booth together. She stopped in her tracks. She told the waiter she changed her mind. He looked at her like she was crazy. "I said I changed my mind." She snapped at him. She stood off to the side and watched Brenda feed James from her plate. She walked to the phone booth and called Vernon. He answered on the first ring. "Hey Vernon this is Vicki, what are you doing?"

"I'm waiting on Brenda slow ass. I been trying not to trip with her but she be doing too much. I made dinner." "Where is Ronnie?"

"She sitting right here in my lap sleep." "Well take her to Shan house and come and meet me at the All You Can Eat Buffet." He started laughing. "I told you I'm waiting on Brenda, I made dinner." "Yeah well I got the feeling she ain't gone be hungry." "Vicki, what the hell are you talking about? Don't try and stir up no shit with me and Brenda, you and Shan need to mind your own business." "Look Vernon, trust me can you just get down here now." She hung up on him. Twenty minutes later he was pulling into the parking lot in his new Bronco.

He pulled into a spot and got out. Vicki grabbed him by the arm and started pulling him into the restaurant. He pulled loose of her grip. "What you drag me down here for Vicki?" She blew an exasperated breath. "Just come in, there is something you need to see." they walked inside and Vicki led Vernon into the direction where Brenda and James were sitting. Brenda was giving James a kiss. Vernon knotted up his face and spoke in a low voice. "Mother mmm, Shan tried to tell me and I just didn't believe her." He walked over to the table and snatched James up by his shirt collar. "James, we suppose to be boys and you gone diss me like this?" He pushed him back into his seat. James stood up, then Brenda stood up and said "Baby wait." James and Vernon looked at her. Vicki could have sworn she seen Brenda smile. Vicki looked at her brother. "Vernon please don't 'do this here. You are causing a scene." He looked around the place and then back at James. All eyes in the place were on him. He Looked at Brenda. "Go get in the truck, and don't even open yo' mouth to say shit to me." She picked up her purse and walked out. Vicki held Vernon by the arm and tried to lead him out. He yanked it out of her grip. "James you better watch yo' punk ass in the streets. You crossed the line fucking with my baby's mama. Game is game but you aint even had to take it there, and we suppose to be boys." He looked at Vicki like he was mad at her and walked out. Vicki watched her brother walk out and she knew he was hurt. She turned around and looked at James and he had the nerve to smile at her. "Sit down Vicki, let me talk to you." She sat down and shook her head at him. "I aint even trying to break up no family and shit Vicki. Brenda told me that she wasn't messing with Vern any more. Said she was just staying there cuz her mama put her and the baby out." Vicki had a look of disgust on her face. "I can't believe that I was ever interested in a looser like you." She stood up and threw a glass of water in his face. She started walking out. She heard him yell, "you loved it, so did yo best friend and yo' sister in law." He started laughing. He wasn't even worth a response.

Vicki drove to Shan house. Ronnie was still there playing with Marcus. Vicki started filling Shan in on what happened. They were laughing when Brenda started beating on Shan's door and yelling for Veronica. "Ronnie come on let's go." Shan got in her face. "Don't be yelling in my house." Veronica and Marcus were standing at the top of the stairs. Vernon came flying across the street. "You aint taking my daughter no where with you ho." He ran up the stairs and picked up Veronica. She looked just like him. He could have birthed her himself. She had big brown eyes like Vernon and tiny doll lips. She was about the color of brown sugar and her eyebrows looked like they could have been arched professionally. He came down the stairs and took her back across the street. Brenda went racing behind him. He went in the house and tried to close the door, but he wasn't quick enough. Vicki and Shan sat in her window and talked while waiting for something to happen. Two wine coolers and a whole lot of laughing past and the front door finally opened. A taxi pulled up with a police car behind it. Brenda came out with a suitcase and Veronica in tow. Shan and Vicki looked at each other, jumped up and ran across the street. Veronica was crying. "I want my daddy." She broke away from Brenda and ran to Vicki. Vicki picked her up. Brenda started yelling. "Put her down Vicki, you and your stupid friend started all of this so now let her go, you aint never gone see her again." Vicki looked over at Vernon who was standing in the doorway. He closed the door. "Auntie Vicki, I want to stay with my daddy." Vicki hugged her real tight. "It's okay you will see him later, go with your mommy now." "No Brenda said he not gone ever see me again and she called the police on him." Brenda started walking towards Vicki but when she seen the look on her face she stopped. Vicki started walking towards Shan house. She heard someone walking up behind her. She was all ready to turn around and slap Brenda. It was the police officer. "Ma'am you need to put her down." Vicki just looked at him. "You need to put her down, she will be leaving with her mother. Please, you are only making it worse for the child." Vicki gave Veronica a tight hug and tried to put her down. She was holding on to Vicki's neck and crying for Vernon. Brenda walked over to Vicki and started pulling on Veronica. She got her loose and they got in the taxi and drove off. Vicki watched in tears as they drove away. This was all her fault.

CHAPTER 21

Two months into a big mess with Vernon and Brenda and Vicki still hadn't heard from Thomas. Loraine was back at Dr. Hardy's office. Vicki was tempted to ask her about her vacation, but she didn't know if it was a good idea. Maybe she was just being paranoid, and she wasn't related to Gloria at all.

At first Vernon wasn't speaking to Vicki. They soon got past that once he started going to court to get full custody of Veronica. He knew it was a long shot, but at least he could get some visitation. Brenda wasn't letting him see her at all. Whenever she said okay, she would call and cancel at the last minute, or not be home. It was awful for Vernon. He really missed his little girl.

Vicki was sitting on her living room floor going over some of her bills. Thomas had paid them before he left but for the last two months Vicki's savings account was practically dry. Vicki noticed a series of calls to New York on her telephone bill. She called the first number. It was the office of Jacobs and Son's. She hung up the phone. She called the second number. It was an answering machine. A man with a deep voice demanded that you leave a message. She hung up. Her head started hurting as she tried to piece together what was going on. She was almost afraid to call the third number. It was too late now, she had to know. She dialed the number with her finger over the mute button. A little girl around Veronica's age answered. "Hello, hello, then she called for her mommy. She knew she hadn't made the calls. Was Eric in her apartment? She started to feel paranoid again. Her mind was racing a mile a minute. Her thoughts were interrupted b a woman who had taken the phone from the little girl. "Hello, is anyone there?" Vicki had to think fast. "I am looking for Eric Matthews, I understand he does contracting outside of his firm. Well my husband and I are looking for a private contractor to design our new home. We were referred to him." There was a silence in the phone and it made Vicki feel uncomfortable. "Hello, is this the right number?" The woman cleared her throat. "Yes this is the right number but Eric is not, well…." "What ever the woman was trying to say she was having a hard time. Vicki was becoming impatient. "What are you talking about Naomi, where is Eric?" "Who the hell is this, how did you know my name? Is this, I know this is not, Victoria, you call my house asking for my husband after you tore our marriage apart?" Vicki was silent, she couldn't speak, but she couldn't hang up. "Eric is not here, he hasn't been here, I haven't heard from him or seen him, okay, he has literally disappeared. Does that make you happy? He could be some where dead for all I know and you have the nerve to call my house and ask for him?" She started crying uncontrollably. Vicki quietly placed the phone back on the hook. She couldn't believe her ears. The man that took her through every emotion was some where missing. That didn't make any sense. This man could possibly be the father of her child and he's no where to be found. She started thinking about how Thomas said he had connections in New York, that he wanted to kill Eric. She couldn't think straight. Her emotions couldn't take all of this turmoil She was taking deep breaths like Dr. Hardy had told her to do when she was getting to over paranoid. The phone ringing startled her. When she answered the phone she sounded like she was out of breath. "Hello" "Vicki, what are you doing, why are you breathing so hard?" "Oh I, uh just walked in I had to run for the phone. Where are you?" "I'm still in Tennessee." "I see." "It's not what you think Listen we need to…" She cut him off. "You don't know what I think…" He cut her off. "Why don't you just listen? I'll be home in about two days. That's Friday. I want you home waiting." Then he hung up. She slammed the phone down and yelled. "Be home waiting, while you got yo' ass in Tennessee with yo wife, oh hell no, you can go to hell Thomas."

All day Friday Vicki was on edge. The time seemed to fly by as she decided what she was going to do. At 4:00 she was going to keep waiting, at 5:30 she was leaving, at 7:20 she decided to just stay home. At 7:30 the phone rang. Vicki just looked at it. She knew it was Thomas. She grabbed her purse and keys and was out the door. After driving around the city for about an hour, she found herself pulling into her mother's driveway. It was 8:30 and the house was completely dark except for the glare of the television. She rang the doorbell and there was no answer. She rang it again and still, no answer. She used her keys and let herself in. Vernon was lying on the couch watching television. Vicki tried to sound cheerful. She went over there to talk about Thomas until she seen how depressed her brother looked. "What's up Vern, you in the house on a Friday night?" "Yeah, I don't feel like being in the street tonight. Plus I was suppose to pick up Veronica today and keep her for the weekend, but of course Brenda faked." "Well you shouldn't let her get to you like this. She is playing with you. Got you stuck in the house on a Friday night waiting, while she's out doing God only knows, with God only knows who." "If there is any chance that I could see my daughter then I am going to push up on it. If I could get her away from Brenda stupid ass and Brenda mama, we not gone even go there. Even for just two days, man. She was supposed to call at 7:00, and well its not really all that late. She might still call." They talked for the next two hours waiting on Brenda to call. She never did. When Vernon called her mother house she said Brenda was gone and hell no Vernon couldn't come get the baby after he threw her and Brenda out in the streets. "Well it's late V, I'm about to head home." "Yeah, I'm a go ahead and get ready for bed I guess. It really aint shit a brother can do until we resolve this in court." They just assume the mother is the better parent." He sucked his teeth. "If only they really knew Brenda." "Well it'll work itself out Vernon, you'll get to see Ronnie real soon." Vernon got up and walked Vicki to the door. They hugged and Vicki walked across the street to Shan's house. "Hey Shan what are you doing home on a Friday night, where is Marcus?" "He's at my cousin house, and shit I'm too old to be running out every weekend." "Shan look, call Vernon. He is having a hard time dealing with this whole Brenda and Veronica thing. Just let him know he has some support, and friends he can lean on." Shan shook her head. "You know I should have beat Brenda ass a long time ago. Now she doing this to Vernon. He knows I have his back. I'll give him a call tomorrow." "All right, look I am about to go home call me from work." Vicki left and got in her car and drove off. She looked in her rearview mirror and saw Shan walking across the street. She smiled all the way home. Shan really has come a long way. She was proud of her best friend.

She was about to go upstairs to her apartment after pulling in to her stall when she though about driving over to

Thomas's house. What if Gloria and the baby were there? She changed her mind. "If I see Thomas it will be him coming to me." She said to herself. She let herself in and was feeling around the wall for the light switch. Somebody grabbed her hand. She screamed, "no Eric don't please." The light came on. "It's not Eric." Vicki was trying to catch her breath. Thomas pulled her into his arms. "I told you before, you aint got to worry about Eric any more. Where have you been, I told you I was coming." She pulled away from him. "You think you could just go away for five, six months and I am suppose to be sitting around on my hands waiting for you to come home. Is this some sort of payback from the past? Well I don't need this, and you know what, I don't need you." He reaches for her but she moved back. "You do need me, and you need to slow your roll before you say something you can't take back." "Thomas you think you can control me, my life, no I take care of myself." "Vicki, I don't want to control you, but I do want to take care of you, protect you." Vicki lost control. "Like you took care of Eric?" Thomas looked down at the floor then took a deep breath and looked back at Vicki. "I don't know what you are talking about Vicki." Vicki couldn't believe Thomas was lying. "Thomas Eric is missing, could be dead, I know you know, and I saw the phone bill you were so eager to pay before you left. I know you and your so-called pull in New York has something to do with it. Thomas you aren't God, you can't just take a man's life." She started crying. "Look Vicki don't cry for that nigga, what ever he got he deserved. I swear, I didn't have anything to do with it. I had some one investigate him find out where he worked and lived. That is it. He owed a lot of people money, made a lot of bad investments. I wasn't the only one looking for him. If he's missing it's because he doesn't want to be found." Vicki didn't know how to respond. "I'm sorry Thomas, I didn't mean to accuse you of anything. There's just so much going on in my life right now." She walked towards him then she heard a strange noise. "Thomas what is that, is that a baby?" He looked towards her bedroom. "That's what I wanted to talk to you about Vicki. If you want to be with me you are going to have to accept my child." Vicki concentrated real hard on the look on Thomas's face. For some reason he looked sad. "Where is

Gloria Thomas? I mean if you are just here because she wants a divorce, well don't do me any favors." He walked into Vicki's room and came out with a baby rapped in a pink blanket. "Vicki, this is my daughter. Natasha Gloria Jones." Vicki just stood there She didn't know how to react. "And where is her mother, you still have not answered me." He started walking towards Vicki with the baby in his arms. Vicki took a step back and was up against the wall. Thomas stood over her holding the baby. "This is my daughter Vicki, hold her." Vicki held out her arms and took the little girl. She was beautiful. She wiggled her body to find comfort in Vicki's arms. "Vicki" Thomas was almost crying when he called her name. "Gloria didn't make it. She died during delivery. That is why I was gone for so long." Vicki covered her mouth with her hand. "Oh Thomas I am so sorry. What are…" He put two fingers up to her lips and said "shhh later".

CHAPTER 22

Thomas and Vicki were late getting to the courthouse to hear the judge's final decision on where Veronica would be living. Natasha had caught a cold and kept them both up all night. Vicki wasn't worried she knew custody was going to be granted to Vernon. If not, he would at least have his fair share of visitation. There would be nothing Brenda could do about that. People sent letters to the family court praising Vernon's ability to raise a child. He was promoted on his job, and he had a steady relationship with a wonderful woman and mother figure. That would be Shan. She was very supportive of Vernon and they became closer than just friends. They were good for each other. The scales were definitely tipped in Vernon's favor. Brenda hardly had a leg to stand on. She was living with her mother in a studio apartment with no job. Living off county checks. She had long since lost her job at Gear Up. She was never coming to work and when she did she was always late. Her mother has been strung out on drugs for years and so far had no intention on cleaning herself up. Vicki almost felt sorry for Brenda, but she had a good thing with Vernon. He was willing and trying to take her away from that sort of life. Provide for her and Veronica a home and a family that cared. Brenda just couldn't handle happiness, or she didn't want it.

She came into court that day wearing a white pants suit and her hair was pulled back in a ponytail. Every one on Vernon side just sort of looked at each other and shrugged. The other times her and the baby came in late and looking like they just crawled out of bed. The one time her mother showed up she was high and they threw her out of the courtroom. Just like usual Veronica broke away from Brenda and ran and sat next to Vernon. Vicki saw the hurt in Brenda's eyes. But what did she expect, she missed her daddy.

After re-hashing all of the testimony from everyone and reading some of the letters sent in on Vernons behalf the judge finally got to the point. He said what everyone knew he would say. Brenda cried through out he whole decision. "Sole, physical and legal custody of Veronica Dupree will be granted to her father Vernon Dupree Jr." There was an outburst of cheers in the courtroom. Veronica even clapped like she knew what was going on. Brenda didn't move she just sat there and continued to cry. "Order, order in my court. Her mother Brenda Knight will be granted every other weekend and alternating holidays. Any other visits will need to be arranged and approved by the father. I trust this will not be a problem Mr. Dupree. I don't want to have to see you back in here with that little girl." Vernon was smiling and holding Veronica. "No sir, not a problem. I will be very fair in allowing her mother to see her. Regardless of how I feel about her." "Very good young man, you are going to be a wonderful father. As for you Ms.Knight, I suggest you enroll in school, or find yourself a job so that you can be a good example to your daughter." Brenda wiped her face with the back of her hand. She didn't respond. "Fine, you are all dismissed."

Things were starting to look up for Vicki and her friends and family. Shan and Marcus had moved in with Vernon and Veronica, just like a little family. Minus the marriage certificate. But according to Shan she was working on that. Vicki and Thomas were making it just fine and she was due any day now. They were on their way to Vernon's house for a Saturday afternoon barbecue. When they arrived Marcus and Veronica were playing in the backyard just like Vicki and Vernon use to do. They got out of the car and Thomas took the baby out of the car seat. Shan was standing on the front porch shielding her eyes from the sun "Hey Vicki, hi Thomas can I hold the baby?' Thomas had only tolerated Shan because she was Vicki's friend. Now she was trying to marry Vernon. He didn't believe a leopard like Shan could change its spots but what was he going to do. Vicki already made it clear that Shan was going to be the godmother of the baby she was about to have. He handed the baby to Shan. "She is so pretty Thomas." He ignored her. "Where is Vernon?" "He's in the back trying to que, you smell burnt chicken don't you?" They all laughed a kind of nervous laugh. Vicki knew Thomas didn't like Shan, but he did promise he would try. He headed towards the backyard with Vernon and the kids. "Shan, you look like a different person, when are you and Vernon having a baby?" Shan started laughing. Girl Vernon is a good man, he has really grown. That experience with Brenda has changed him. He makes me want to be a better person and mother you know.

But just to the ones we have, I aint tryna' go there without no ring." Vicki started to laugh, and then all of a sudden she buckled over holding her stomach. She screamed real loud. Vernon, Thomas and the kids came running from the backyard. Thomas rushed over to Vicki. She stood up and took a deep breath. She closed her eyes and calmly said. "I'm in labor." Her water broke. Veronica and Marcus started laughing and pointing saying she peed on herself. Thomas was looking dazed and scared. Shan spoke first. "Thomas, I will watch Natasha and me and Vernon will meet you up at the hospital. You and Vicki should leave now." He didn't speak; he just walked over to the passenger door and let Vicki in. They took off for the hospital. Vernon, Shan and the kids were right behind them. Thomas was so nervous. There were so many complications with Gloria, he wasn't even allowed in the delivery room. He was standing at the top of Vicki's bed rubbing her shoulders and her back. He felt bad for her having to go through all of this pain. The doctor was encouraging her to push. Push harder, I see a head." Vicki grunted and pushed and screamed. She dug her nail into Thomas's arm. "Come on

Victoria keep pushing." She pushed and kept holding on to Thomas arm. "It's almost out, it's a boy." Vicki fell back against the pillows and tried to catch her breath. "You can cut the cord if you like sir." Thomas walked to the end of the bed and cut the cord that tied Vicki to the baby. The baby was rinsed and wrapped in a blanket. The nurse handed the screaming baby boy to Vicki and he stopped crying.

Thomas walked out of the room and announced, it's a boy. Vernon hugged him and told him congratulations. He went in to see Vicki and his new nephew. Shan stood there holding Natasha and looking at Thomas. He reach for his daughter. "It's all good Shan, you're a god mother now go see your new god son." She smiled at Thomas and handed him his daughter. He hugged his daughter and held her close to his face. He whispered to her. "They made it, they made it."

That night Thomas couldn't sleep. Every time he closed his eyes he imagined that when his son opened his eyes they were going to be green. Thomas couldn't get over how pale the little boy was. As dark as he was and Vicki's caramel colored skin, he felt like the boy should have some color. His daughter had come out brown, and was almost his color. Vicki could hear something was wrong in Thomas voice when she called him last night. She knew exactly what he was thinking. "Thomas don't worry, he'll get some color. Let's just go ahead and have the blood test so we can move on with what ever decisions need to be made." "I'm just kind of tired Vicki, and over whelmed, I'm not tripping. I don't need a test to know he's mine." Thomas reminded himself of the conversation he had with Vicki last night on the way to the hospital. He wanted to be in good spirits when he picked her and the baby up. When he walked into the room the baby was lying in a plastic hospital bassinet. Vicki was coming out of the bathroom moving slowly as an old woman. "Can you rap him up Thomas, we can go home now." He took a deep breath and picked up the baby. He stared at him long and hard. The baby stretched and yawned. Thomas started smiling at him. His previous feelings was quickly being erased with each second he held him. The boy started fluttering his eyes, and then they opened. Abroad smile crossed Thomas's face as he stared down into the face of the brown-eyed baby. He held him close to his chest and whispered in his ear. "You had to let daddy know, huh, you gone be a genius boy." Vicki watched Thomas from the bathroom, she felt so proud. He kissed his son and looked over at Vicki standing in the bathroom door. He blew her a kiss and said "Thank you"

About the Author

Born and raised in San Francisco, R.L. Coats is the middle child of eight children. She currently works and resides in the city of Oakland, California. where she is working on her second novel *Friends Like These*.